Adam
and
Eve
and
Pinch-Me

Adam
and
Eve
and
Pinch-Me

JULIE JOHNSTON

Tundra Books

First published in Canada by Lester Publishing, Ltd, Toronto, 1994
First published in the United States by Little, Brown and Company,
New York, 1994
First published in this edition by Tundra Books, Toronto, 2003

Published in Canada by Tundra Books,
481 University Avenue, Toronto, Ontario M5G 2E9

Published in the United States by Tundra Books of Northern New York,
P.O. Box 1030, Plattsburgh, New York 12901

Library of Congress Control Number: 2003100909

National Library of Canada Cataloguing in Publication

Johnston, Julie, 1941-
   Adam and Eve and Pinch-me / Julie Johnston.

ISBN 0-88776-648-X

   I. Title.

PS8569.O387A43 2003   jC813'.54   C2003-900703-0
PZ7

We acknowledge the financial support of the Government of Canada
through the Book Publishing Industry Development Program and
that of the Government of Ontario through the Ontario Media
Development Corporation's Ontario Book Initiative. We further
acknowledge the support of the Canada Council for the Arts and the
Ontario Arts Council for our publishing program.

Design: Cindy Elisabeth Reichle
Printed and bound in Canada

1 2 3 4 5 6   08 07 06 05 04 03

For Diane and Doug, Kathie and Malcolm

ACKNOWLEDGMENTS

I wish to thank Robert Penny and Murray McMunn for generously answering my many questions.

Adam
and
Eve
and
Pinch-Me

CHAPTER

1

Just shut up. I'd like to tell my brain to just shut up. Have you ever noticed how you can't make your mind stop thinking even though you try to think about absolutely nothing? You still keep on thinking about how you're trying to think about nothing because you want to avoid thinking about the thing you don't want to think about? Oh, shut up.

I appear to be talking to a machine.

I can blank out people. Wipe them right off the board. Paint over them. Close the book on them. Click, erase, gone. It's me I'm having trouble escaping. A computer is very close to perfection. I love the way you can press cancel or delete and it actually happens. To the printed word, that is.

I'm leaving this place. Mrs. K. and Frank are past tense. It's not breaking my heart to leave because as a ward of the Children's Aid I'm used to it. Any idea what that means? Not bloody likely.

Here's a hint. What do you do with something you don't want? Throw it out, of course. And what do you call the junk you throw out? You got it.

I'm losing it, obviously. Do I expect this machine to give answers?

My new address will be: Sara Moone, c/o E. Huddleston, RR 3, Ambrose, Ontario. An easy address compared to this one: c/o Mrs. Avartha Koscyzstin, 319 Campagnola Street East, North Malverington, Ontario. And let's see, what was the one before that? Station Road. No number. That was the Lomers, I think. The only thing I remember about that place was, Arn never laid a hand on us kids. He made us memorize that statement. Sonia, his wife, got slapped around on a regular basis, however.

I have no idea exactly how many foster homes I've been in. I was in a group home once and hated it more than anything. Kids kept stealing my stuff. I hide everything now, money especially. Having my own money is very important to me.

A lot of cruelty went on in that place. One of the older kids broke my finger by tricking me. "Put your finger in the crow's nest," he said, "the crow's not at home." So, like a sucker, I stuck my finger into his big, crunching fist. My finger's still crooked. I used to get sucked in by Adam and Eve and Pinch-Me, too. Until I found out the right answer.

Don't plan on digesting my whole life story here, because I've forgotten most of it. And what I remember would bore the brains out of a dead cow. I came to stay with Mrs. K. (everybody calls her Mrs. K., including Frank, her elderly husband) when I was about thirteen. I'm fifteen now. That's the longest I've stayed anywhere. I'll be sixteen at the end of August and then *kaboom*. I start living. No more social workers. No more foster parents. No more school. I will be me, alone, untouchable.

I'd better start packing. They took Mrs. K. off to the hospital about an hour ago, although she wasn't supposed to have her operation until next month. "I'm a bit sickly," she always said to me. Sickly! She's been at death's door since day one. There were times when I wouldn't have minded nudging her right through it. I've been playing nursemaid here for the past year and a half, almost. Oh well, so what? It's February, which means only six months left in limbo. I can hardly wait to start my life.

I've got everything packed except this machine. One suitcase and one cardboard box hold the contents of my so-called existence. Another cardboard box contains my books. My other existences. I've got my money pinned to my underwear. Frank said he'd carry down my stuff. I said forget it. The stuff weighs more than he does. Especially the books. Frail old Frank, sitting down there by the window in his La-Z-Boy, waiting for Ruth to pick me up so he can go and sit in a chair at the hospital and listen to Mrs. K. belch and moan about how sickly she is. "I'll be along later, love," he said to her. Love! How pathetic!

However, I will say this about old Frank, he's generous. "Take the computer with you," he said.

I said, "You're kidding!"

3

"Why would I be kidding?" he said. He's just retired and the place where he used to work bought all new computers so he got a deal on this old one. "Maybe you'll relate to it, because, God knows, you don't relate to people." Suddenly he's a psychologist. Frank Freud. I hate that. I hate when people think they have you figured out. Of course I don't relate to people. Why would I? I'm not related to anybody and nobody's related to me.

Ruth insists this is not true. ShutupshutupshutUP.

Forget it. That's what I don't want to think about. Ruth's here. I have to unplug this thing and lug it out to her car. She's my case worker and will be driving me to my new foster home. I'm pressing exit. Yes I'll save this. Temporarily.

O give me a home where the imbeciles roam – I can't believe this place. A farm! They've placed me at some kind of a farm. Am I being punished? Do they think I have animalistic tendencies? I mean, look! I've never done anything wrong in my life. I obey every rule in the book. The way to get along in this world is be invisible. Flatten yourself out and wait. That's what I thought I was doing. Just hanging around blending in with the wallpaper, waiting until my sixteenth birthday. I thought it was my darkest hour when I ended up with Mrs. K. and Frank exuding compassion for the homeless in their house haunted by every cabbage they'd ever boiled in their lives. They went in for boiled fish, too, and deeply waxed floors and they were death on open windows. But this place!

Actually the house *smells* okay. It smells like the inside of a bakery, which is not too hard to take. Outside is a different story. They insisted on showing me a bunch of beady-eyed chickens and a barn full of decaying sheep. When I held my nose, they laughed and said I'd get used to it. I said, "Don't bet on it," but they didn't hear me. I have this affliction. When I talk to strangers, I sound as though I'm trying out my voice for the first time.

These people have some kind of a mangy old dog that sidled up to me and put its head under my hand. I mean, what was I supposed to do? I'm no great lover of animals, but it seems a natural reaction to pat a dog's head if it's right there under your hand. "Don't pat the dog!" somebody yelled at me. "Is this a n-n-n-nut house?" I tried to ask them, my other affliction making its presence known.

"N-n-no, it's the loony b-b-bin!" shrieked this jerk-ass kid, who ran before I could grab him and tear the living mouth right off his face.

But wait. I'll go back to this afternoon. Ruth and I clunking along in her car heading out of town. No heater. Weather cold as a witch's tit. Slithering around icy corners. No treads on the tires. Me, minding my own business, not saying anything, even though Ruth is one of the few people I can talk to without sounding as though cracker crumbs are stuck in my throat, and looking out through a little patch on my window I'd defrosted with my bare fist. I was watching the houses peter out until there was nothing left but field after snowy field of nothingness. Ruth said, "How do you feel about moving to a new place?"

"Okay," I said. She tried to give me one of those in-depth eye-contact looks but gave it up when we started to go into a skid. She was managing to get enough warm air blowing onto the windshield to give her an egg-shaped view. She decided to look at the road.

"How do you feel about leaving the Koscyzstin's?"

"Okay," I said.

"It's too bad about Mrs. K. If we could have avoided this move we would have, but the situation looked pretty hopeless. I'm sorry about your friends."

"Friends?"

"You'll miss your school buddies."

"Oh. Right." The best way to handle Ruth is tell her what she wants to hear. She's spent her entire adult life picking over misery, sorting out disasters, trying to bring a little joy into people's lives. Why burden her with my lack of friends?

"Are you happy, Sara?"

"Intensely." She was trying to look at me again, so I gave her my Little-Orphan-Annie look. Like the comic strip character with zeros for eyes?

We drove along, leaving the flat fields behind, and started chugging up and down some serious hills. The road narrowed and became lined with trees. A wall of trees. We were surrounded, boxed in, by some kind of primeval forest. Deep, impenetrable, hostile. Ruth was still going on about my friends and wanting me to talk about myself. I told her I thought I was coming down with laryngitis. What's there to tell, anyway? She must have a file

6

describing the vital statistics of Sara Moone, height, weight, etcetera. All she has to do is look me up on her computer if she wants to know what I'm like. What she sees is what I am. Tallish. Thinnish. Reddish of hair. Distinguishing features? None. No, maybe they keyed in burn scars, left leg. That sums up Sara Moone.

Ruth didn't believe I was coming down with laryngitis. "Tell me about your school friends," she said.

If I've learned one thing in my life it's this: if you don't want your heart broken, don't let on you have one. It's the motto I live by. It allows me to keep my personality flat. No heart, no brains, no guts. At school this girl who sat in front of me in computer class asked me over to her house one day. At first my insides started knotting up, and I thought I'd puke right in front of her until I remembered I had no guts. "C-can't," I said and walked away. How could I? What would be the point? The girl would find out that I had about as much substance as a dropped ice cube, that I wasn't based on anything, and that would be the end of it. I'm disposable. "Can't make it," I always say. I don't make excuses; I never aim for a soft little smile of regret. I am so incredibly cool it's becoming my trademark. I only have one problem. After I say no, after I turn people down, just seconds later, I sometimes think I have become solidified, fixed. One of my foster things once yelled at me, "Your face is gonna freeze like that!" I think I was trying to look like an attack dog with rabies. Frozen. That's the way I feel after I say no. I've become frozen – in a negative position. Then the feeling goes and I can move.

Ruth was still waiting for me to tell her about my friends. "A fun-loving and loyal group," I said. She shook her head and frowned into the darkening afternoon. It was starting to snow. Sherwood forest was easing up a bit. The road ran crookedly between pink slabs of rock. It could have been chiseled piece by piece out of the hill by some sculptor obsessed by a single idea: Get to the other side! Find a way through!

"I'm not trying to pry, you know," Ruth said. "I just want to get to know you a little bit better. What do you do when you're not in school?"

"Drugs." I was making another peephole with the palm of my hand, but I sensed by the way we slid into another skid that she was looking at me instead of the road. "Kidding," I said. I was, too. Only dimwits and emotional screwups do drugs. Fortunately, I am neither.

I could see a few scrubby farms, now, poked into the frosty hills, some with lights on as if they were expecting someone to drop in. Or hoping.

"Seriously," she said, "do you have any hobbies?"

"A little embroidery now and then. Paint-by-numbers. Candy striping."

"I said seriously."

"Teaching Sunday school."

"Sara!"

"Of course I don't have any hobbies. What do you take me for?"

At the Koscyzstin's, I used to spend weekend after blank weekend just sitting around listening for Mrs. K.'s next feeble request and waiting for time to pass. I admit I did a lot of reading – everything I could lay my hands on, novels, magazines, newspapers, cereal boxes. I get involved in books to the point where it becomes embarrassing. When I read *The Secret Garden*, I began to sound quite snotty. When I read *The Color Purple*, I developed a southern drawl. I'm not safe around books.

Sometimes I spend time studying, not to pull off high marks, which I get whether I study or not, but because I like knowing things. Knowing things will allow me to survive when I start my life. That and money.

Mrs. K. was never what you'd call a robust woman, up and down with one ailment or another over most of those two years. "Do you think you could come straight home after school?" she'd say with her voice one notch away from a whine. "I couldn't get up the steam to start hoovering the rugs at all yesterday, and they're just thick." Or she'd say, "Don't make any plans for Saturday, I've a list for you a mile long. It just gives me the pip thinking about it." She'd sit there casting her gloomy eye on me, rubbing her belly. And then she'd ease out these long and mournful belches. "Now stay within earshot, Sara," she used to say. "You never know when I might need something from the drug store."

But big deal, so what? Being bogged down with household chores didn't kill me. I got kind of used to running errands and carrying bowls of pale soup and plates of dry toast to her. I'm not complaining. I didn't exactly feel sorry for the old girl. I felt sort of . . . responsible. Who else did she have? Frail Frank? Anyway, why would I need friends cluttering up my present life? Reality starts at sixteen.

Picture me as something like a little hyphen on a blank screen. A cursor. Unattached to anything before or after. I move along and down, along and down, until finally I get to page sixteen. That's when the story starts. Me, alone, in a very sturdy, very compact, glass fortress where I can see out but no one can see beyond the surface. Queen of cool. Of course I'll need a job because I haven't been able to save much money, but I'm not fussy. Night watchman at the morgue would suit me fine.

My real dream is this: I'm going up north, as far north as I can go and still get a job, some remote outpost where I'll have my own space unshared by any other human being. I might have a dog. One of those Huskies, intelligent and loyal. I would like to be a pilot who flies supplies into even more remote places.

"I think you'll like the Huddlestons'," Ruth said. "There are other kids there. A ready-made family for you."

No clutter. No noise. No responsibilities.

"Two boys younger than you."

"O joy divine." I took off my glove again and pressed my hand against my side of the windshield to broaden my horizons. Nothing to see except angry snowflakes attacking horizontally and disappearing. The road was becoming narrower and more twisted. We were beyond the boonies. Way beyond. "Turn on your headlights," I said.

"They're on."

I've never driven a car, but I know I could do it. Ruth,

on the other hand, seems to have skipped driver's ed. She was intent on putting us in the ditch. She kept turning the wheel too far coming out of a skid, which any damn fool knows – But who cares? I didn't.

Ruth glanced at me a couple of times as if she had something important to say but didn't know how to start. Finally, she said, "I'm not trying to pressure you, but couldn't you agree to read one letter from your mother? It's been over a year now since she contacted us, looking for you. You're under no obligation to answer it. But maybe you should give her half a chance to prove herself. You're prejudging her."

"She prejudged me."

"Oh, stop. You know as well as I do how many reasons there are for a woman to give up a baby."

"None of them good, if you happen to be the baby. Ex-baby."

"You were adopted immediately. You know that."

"I don't remember. Anyway, big deal. They died."

"Sara. They didn't do it on purpose."

"I didn't say they did."

"Well, you sound so – The fire was a tragic accident. It wasn't anyone's fault. No one set out to deprive you, personally, of a home and a family. It was one of those things."

"I'm not really interested in pursuing this any further."

Ruth heaved one of her big, dramatic sighs as if she were going to let the subject drop. But no. "I really should confess," she said, "that your mother knows you are moving to the Ambrose area."

"How come? Is there some sort of conspiracy against me? Why are you trying to spoil my life?"

"I didn't do it," Ruth said. "But I'm afraid the information got leaked out by mistake. We had temporary help for a while – and the woman *is* persistent. The last time she contacted me she said she intended to ask everyone in the whole county, if necessary, to track down the family who had adopted her daughter."

"What's her point?"

"Your well-being, I gather. She wants to see if you're happy, and to let you know she's out there. Seems harmless enough."

I stared into the ranks of snowflakes driving against the windshield and tried to make out a formation, some pattern, but it only made me dizzy. "Wait a minute," I said. "I'm not adopted. She's looking for some kid who's adopted, and that ain't me." I smiled. Safe. Anonymous. "Right?"

Ruth glanced at me and we narrowly missed a snow-bank. "You might want a mother someday."

"I'll be the judge of that. What does this woman look like?" If I was going to be involved in some kind of cloak-and-dagger chase, I needed a running start. Ruth didn't know, as it turned out, nor did the woman have a picture of me.

I do have one thing, however, which I've never told anyone about. The ad.

Sitting beside Ruth, I returned to my dream of being sixteen, of splitting off, separating myself from people.

All people. What I want is sole control of Sara Moone, because up to now my life has had no more importance to anyone than a scrap of paper, scribbled on, torn up, thrown away, burned to an ash. I have never had a say in what happens to me. When I was eight, my foster mother at the time became pregnant with twins. She sat me down for a heart-to-heart talk about this. I was so excited about the twin babies we were going to have that I didn't hear her tell me that she was giving me back to the Children's Aid. I was grinning away like an idiot, thinking about how I'd get to feed the babies their bottles, and she was saying, "I'm very sorry, I don't know what else I can do." And things like that. And I just stood there when it finally sank in, my lips frozen in a wide stretch across my face and my eyes turning into round empty circles. In my next home, my foster mother was ruled unfit and the family fell apart. Then there was another one, and another, until I stopped being able to sort them out. I've been plucked up, plunked down, shuffled and re-dealt so many times my mind refuses to remember it all.

However, sixteen is the magic age. That's when I can legally drop out of school, legally drop out of foster homes . . . and legally drop off the edge of the world, I guess, for all anyone would care.

"I really care what happens to you, you know," Ruth said. She looked at me quickly and then back at the road. We were at the top of a long, slow grade lightly dusted with snow. "You could write to me."

"And say what?"

"Tell me how you feel about things, about what your life is like. You have that computer; you might as well put it to good use."

"Can't. I don't have a printer. Even if I did, it wouldn't do you any good. I don't feel anything about anything, so you'd get nothing but blank pages." Actually I was beginning to feel us going into a slide down this hill. Ruth felt it, too, and hit the brakes. We did a slow-motion, complete spin and drifted off the road nose-first into the ditch.

"Oh, great," Ruth said.

"Any survivors?" I said.

She tried gunning the engine. The wheels spun uselessly. "What are we going to do? We're miles from anywhere." Her purse was on the seat between us. She opened it and started rummaging around. She took out a package of cigarettes and a lighter.

The inside of the car seemed incredibly small all of a sudden. "What are you doing?"

She started lighting her cigarette. "Do you mind?"

The lighter was turned up too high. I could see her face, her eyes questioning mine, wondering if I minded her smoking, but hoping I didn't because she needed to smoke, and her hair, pale brown, like dried grass, wisping out from under her green knitted hat toward the flame. The way the flame flared up, I don't know, I guess it made me panic. I may have screamed. I yelled, anyway, because Ruth jumped and her cigarette flipped out from between her fingers. I saw a rain of sparks in front of the flare from the lighter and I – Forget it.

I got out of the car. Smoke inside a car is sickening.

I remember Ruth running after me. The two of us standing in the middle of snowy nowhere shouting at each other. She tried to put her arm around me, but I gave her a shove and then the bus came along. Out of the white screen of blowing snow, headlights. And Ruth sprawled on the road in its path. One instant Ruth was lit up and the next she was in semi-darkness as the bus's headlights swerved from side to side down that glassy hill with the tortured sound diesel brakes have drowning out everything else. I grabbed her arm and yanked her into the ditch as the bus crunched past and came to a stop a little farther along the road.

It's fairly quiet here, now, at Château Huddleston, except for me clicking away on this machine. Supper was a major ordeal. Food has never been a big item in my life. Here, however, quantity is everything. God knows what the quality is like. I didn't eat enough of whatever was being served to tell. After they'd all sucked back about forty tons of unidentifiable, gravy-covered, cooked objects, they paused long enough to breathe and looked at my plate, still brimful. "Edith-Ann will like it," someone said. Whoever that is. Probably some idiot daughter locked in the attic. This would not be entirely out of the question.

The lord of the manor has retired as has his charming wife. The two delightful foster sons have gone beddy-bye in the room next to mine after surgically removing each other's windpipes, I gather. They were fighting over a jackknife and then one of them started choking and coughing until Ma (can you dig it?) Huddleston put a stop to it. "And no dessert for three days," she said. I can't believe this place.

I see I left off when the bus came along. I was interrupted. No such thing as privacy around here.

To go back: It was the Ottawa bus and we got on. Ruth told the driver where we were going and he said that was his next stop. Sitting beside each other in the last two seats on the bus, we didn't have a whole lot to say. Pressed close to the window, I looked out. The snow had stopped coming down and was just blowing around now. I'd already told Ruth I was sorry. I was, too. I hadn't meant to shove her under a bus. I'm cool, but I'm no murderer. "I'm sorry, too," she'd said. "I should have remembered that you don't like to be touched."

Elbows tucked into my rib cage, legs tight against the bus heater, I ignored her remark. Through the bus window I watched the clouds part, revealing the moon, a mean little curved blade slung low in the darkening sky. It was following us.

Fifteen minutes later the bus pulled into the Elite Cafe and Bus Terminal on the edge of the town of Ambrose. "You go inside there," the bus driver said to Ruth as we stepped down out of the bus into the snowy bluster. "They'll call you a tow truck and you can get a coffee while you wait." The bus door eased to, then snapped closed, and the bus disappeared into a turmoil of exhaust and snow.

We looked at each other and shrugged. You could hardly see in through the windows, they were so fogged up. Inside, the warmth of the place almost wrapped itself around us with steam coming up from pots of coffee behind the counter and a frazzle-haired waitress filling the cups of a few old geezers sitting on stools gabbing their heads off, their big coats hanging open. Fluorescent lights beat down on them like a sunny day. A couple of tables stood empty under the windows. I slid into a chair beside one and waited for Ruth to ask the waitress about a tow truck.

Everybody stopped talking to listen in. "Where am I phoning from?" Ruth called to the waitress from the pay phone on the wall. "Ee-lite Cafe out on the number seven. He knows where it is."

"Not a night to be out on the road," one of the patrons of the Ee-lite Cafe said to no one in particular.

"That skiffle o' snow on top o' the glare ice just slicks her down good," someone else said.

"D'y' mind the time we froze up after a long thaw and we were froze up so good there wasn't hardly a toilet'd flush in the entire county? Two year ago now, it was."

"It wasn't neither. It was last spring."

Ruth went back to the counter to get change for another call and they all shut up again.

"Mr. Huddleston?" Ruth was saying into the phone. "Ruth Petrie from the Children's Aid. I wonder if you could come into the Elite, uh, Ee-lite Cafe to pick up Sara. I've put my car in the ditch." A pause. "Your foster daughter. Sara Moone."

Meanwhile I was cringing, trying to disappear into the furniture. Obviously I hadn't been programmed into Mr. Huddleston's memory. When I looked up all I could see was a row of eyes staring at me from the mirror above the counter. I turned to the window but I couldn't see out.

"Yes." Relief in her voice. "Yes, that's right."

The software must have kicked in.

After she hung up, Ruth got us both coffee and then she went to the washroom. There was a general buzz of conversation, some of which I caught.

"Bears for punishment, aren't they."

"Oh, I don't know. Hud, he's got a firm hand there."

"Missus is a bit soft."

"A bit soft. Salt o' the earth, though."

"Oh, salt o' the earth, no question. But why they keep takin' in them kids, I'll never tell y'."

"Bears for punishment."

*T*omorrow, and tomorrow, and tomorrow, creeps in this petty pace – Good Lord, it's come to this. Quoting Shakespeare fergawdsake. I am so endlessly bored.

When I first got here, Ma could hardly wait to show me my room. Hanging on the wall of this – enclosure – was a piece of embroidery, framed. The words on it said "Sugar 'n Spice 'n Everything Nice," and in one corner a little girl in a bonnet peeped coyly out at me. Throw-up material! Ma spent the next half hour telling me how she had spotted this kit at a yard sale and all you had to do was pick out some nice colored yarn and do the needlework and then fit it into the frame and she just had to have it even though she didn't have a girl and then next day didn't she find out she was getting a girl and isn't that always the way because you just never know . . . blah, blah, and blah. That's the way she talks.

When she finally went out, I turned it to the wall.

I get up in the morning to the sound of Ma's constant conversation interspersed with the radio news, weather, and sports. Heard over all this is Josh, aged four, yelling, "Gimme!" or some other endearing command, and Nick, I don't know how old he is, he's small for his age but looks older than his size, Nick, weaseling around, sucking up to Ma and whining about one of his pancakes being burned. Pancakes! I can't believe the food around here. Ma's life is focused on feeding us. She doesn't eat much herself. Doesn't stop talking long enough. She's not in any danger of fading away, however. She's short but hefty. A little square woman.

And then there's Hud. Not much to say about Hud. A big guy. Looks like he could pick up one corner of the house and set it down again without straining his back. His face must be permanently tanned. It looks a bit like a wood carving with all the lines and creases he has.

This morning Ma looked up from the frying pan when Hud came into the kitchen and started in: "Now, you just get yourself sitting down at the table sure those ewes'll hang on another half hour without you out there cluckin' over 'em like somethin' halfway between a mother hen and a midwife and not a bite o' breakfast down your gullet for you could starve to death and never keel over till somebody told you you were stone cold do you want ketchup mixed up in your eggs or just on top the hens are starting to lay."

"Yep," Hud said.

Hud, it seems, is a man of single syllables. Ma mixed ketchup in with his scrambled eggs and then dumped more on top.

School is a welcome relief. Being new is like being invisible. People don't like to get too friendly around here until they have you figured out. I intend to remain inscrutable. I only wish I didn't have to go by school bus. The first day I went, Nick looked as if he was going to sit beside me, so I quickly plunked my knapsack into the seat and said, "It's taken." He moved on. About three stops later, the bus was filling up and across from the Elite Cafe some guy got on and stood beside my knapsack. He didn't even ask if the seat was taken, just dumped it in my lap and sat down. Jerk. He wears glasses. He's ahead of me in school, about ready to graduate, probably.

A few days later he did the same thing. Also the day after that.

Saturdays are deadly. It's the beginning of March. Hardly any snow left on the road but still plenty in the fields. I took the Huddlestons' excuse for a bicycle, a relic of the fifties, complete with a wooden crate fastened above the back wheel, to ride into the Elite Cafe and Bus Terminal to pick up a package Ruth said she would send me by bus. Books. One about the far north, which she said was a gift, also an atlas I can keep, and another one about bush pilots that she borrowed from a friend and wants back.

Josh, the little guy, doesn't like to see anybody going anywhere without him. Unfortunately, he saw me get the bike out, and before I could even get the thing down the driveway, he was stumbling after me. At the road I hopped on and started pedaling fast.

"Hey! Wait up! You heard me! Wait up!"

I looked back and saw this half-pint general in an over-sized snowsuit, ramrod stiff, bellowing commands. I pedaled on down the hard-packed dirt road to the highway, blocking out the sound of his voice by concentrating on the frozen ruts threatening to sabotage the balloon tires of the bike. He ran after me for a bit but must have stopped to stamp on the iced-over puddles. When I paused at the stop sign, I could hear the ice splinter. "I'm telling," he wailed.

I didn't want to look back, but that feeling of becoming solidified was creeping over me. I had to make sure I could still turn my head, so I glanced over my shoulder. Josh stood there in the middle of the road with his mittens dangling by strings out of his coat sleeves. At first I thought he was grinding his grubby fists into his eyes because he was crying. But it wasn't that. I think he was wagging one finger on each hand in my direction. Preserve me from the lunatic fringe.

I turned up the collar of my jacket over my ears, which were beginning to get nipped, and took off. I don't like the kid. Why would I? I don't hate him or anything, I just don't like him. One more kid whose mother doesn't want him. Big deal.

I flipped Josh out of my mind and pedaled faster, even though I could scarcely see with the wind making my eyes water and my lashes freeze. The sound of his voice was getting on my nerves.

At the Elite Cafe I propped the Huddlestons' bike

against the peeling paint. The Ottawa bus had just pulled into the paved area in front of the cafe. From under the overhang I watched a couple of people getting off the over-heated bus into the rawness of March, hunching down into their coat collars. A young woman with a baby got off and was met by an older woman with a car. There was a lot of hugging and kissing there, and squealing on the part of the baby. An old man nearly lost his balance, but the bus driver put out a steadying hand to save him. A tallish, thin-nish woman got off and gawked around as if she'd just landed on some planet not Earth. She waited beside the bus for the driver to get her suitcase out of the hold. Then the bus driver took two cardboard boxes and a brown paper-wrapped package into the cafe. I followed him in.

"Three pickups for you, Fran."

"I'll get to them when I get a minute. Busier than a one-armed paperhanger, today."

"Take'er easy." He put the packages on the end of the counter near the cash register and left. Fran, behind the counter, nodded her permed head at the bus driver, acknowledging the packages.

The usual coffee drinkers were on hand. Must be their home away from home. I sat on a stool at the end of the counter to avoid sitting next to a bulgy lady brushing muffin crumbs off her bosom into her coffee.

"Hey, Babe! Lend me some money, I'll buy y'a Coke." Nick, the pride and joy of Huddleston Heights, had wormed his way in between me and Madam Bulgy. He twinkled his eyes at me as if we shared a joke.

"Thought they kept you on a short leash." I said it fast and low to avoid sounding like a strangled crow. Nick had been confined to the Huddlestons' property for two weeks for some crime he'd committed. I don't pay attention to what goes on in that place, so I don't know what it was. Hitchhiking somewhere and staying out all night. Something like that. Pity he hadn't stayed permanently. I like him even less than I like Josh. I gather he's been with the Huddlestons a long time, at least by my measurement of time in a placement.

"Great leash! The old lady forgot to tie the other end."

The customers in the cafe were beginning to look at us. I let the conversation lapse. In the mirror behind the counter I watched Nick toss back half his Coke as if he'd been memorizing whiskey-drinking gangsters in B-grade movies. His twinkle hardened into a leer as he dragged his arm across his mouth. I gave him what I consider my hardboiled look, got off my stool, and moved to the other end of the counter. I stood near the packages.

I've only known Nick a few weeks, but I know his type. If he can't be number one in your dreams, he wants to be number one in your nightmares. Things happen when he's around, but nothing's ever his fault. I've run across a few people like him over the years. Remorseless. Shed their crimes like a skin and slink back smoother than ever. I've read articles in magazines about "problem teens." Insecure. Low self-esteem. Blah, blah. Words. Ruth goes on about things like that, too, only her favorites are dysfunctional and maladjusted. I always think she's talking about machinery.

Nick followed me to the other end of the counter and took the stool next to the cash register. He put down his glass with a bang as if he owned the space. The problem with Nick is, he seems to think the world is spread out just for him to spoil. For example, yesterday I found that bloody awful dog on my bed. It's barely smart enough to find its way into the house, let alone open my bedroom door and close it behind him. And the stink. Something like bad breath and dirty laundry gone mildewed combined. I yelled at it and it slunk out as if I'd taken a club to it. Downstairs I started telling Ma, and the damn thing came up and put its head under my hand, begging to be patted. Ma interrupted her spiel about how Edith-Ann (Edith-Ann!!) prefers to live in the barn and has to be coaxed into the house if they want it in, which they usually don't because of the smell, and somebody must have dragged it in with a rope because it's as stubborn as an old goat and smells like one too . . . "Don't pat the dog!" She emphasized this last, so I backed away. "That Nick," she said. "One of his practical jokes, no doubt."

No doubt whatsoever. I had to wash my top blanket and my pillow case.

I stood there waiting to get my package, ignoring Nick, hoping he'd go away. The woman who had got off the bus came in with her suitcase and put it down behind Nick's stool. She put a twenty-dollar bill on the counter and asked Fran, the waitress, for change for the phone. "With ya in a sec, honey bun," Fran said. "One or two payin' customers 'heada ya."

The woman left the bill on the counter, unbuttoned her coat, and looked around. In the mirror she saw me staring at her and stared back. I looked down at the packages the bus driver had left. One was addressed to me. The books. The woman said to Fran, "Is Bellcroft Manor very far from here?"

Everybody at the counter had stopped talking by now, and they were all giving the woman the once-over.

Suddenly her suitcase, behind Nick, fell over. Everyone watched as she bent to pick it up. I didn't. I shot out a hand, and like a vise, I had Nick by the back of his scrawny neck. I squeezed until he let go of the twenty on the counter. I know the value of money, even when it's somebody else's.

We were surrounded by eyes then. Fran's (she knew instantly what had happened), the woman's (she didn't), and the customers' (they weren't sure but suspected treachery of some sort). Nick glared a threat at my reflection in the mirror and then looked coolly into his glass.

The woman had to ask her question again.

"Bellcroft Manor?" Fran cocked up one eyebrow, thinking.

Madam Bulgy said, "She must mean Bellingtons'."

"That'd be Bellingtons'," a man with earflaps hanging like an apron around his peaked cap repeated.

The woman said, "It's a bed and breakfast. I've booked a room there."

"What the Sam Hill's a bed and breakfast?" somebody halfway along the counter asked. He honked his fat nose into a well-used handkerchief.

The woman told Fran she wanted to phone a taxi to take her to this place.

"If it's Bellingtons' you're going to, it's only across the road and along. Not worth the taxi coming all the way out. Just phone over and the young lad'll come and get you." She handed her a quarter out of the till, but the woman tapped her twenty on the counter. "Skip it," Fran said. "Phone's on the house."

"I always pay my way," she said and pushed her money toward Fran.

"Whatever snaps yer gum," Fran said and gave her her change.

When she began to dial the phone on the wall opposite the counter, the patrons of the Ee-lite Cafe ran out of conversation. All ears were cocked in the direction of the telephone. The earflap man was probably hard of hearing, because he creaked right around on his stool trying to lip-read. The woman turned her back to the audience and kept her voice low. After she'd hung up, she moved her suitcase and sat down at one of the little empty tables. She stared at the steamed-up window, rubbed a little section, and looked out.

"You want coffee?" Fran called over to her.

"No thanks."

"Doughnut?"

"Nothing."

The general buzz started up again. Nick was gone. His glass sat empty on the counter. I watched Fran check the packages from the bus, tear off bits of paper, and add a hasty scrawl to a ledger. I reached out for mine and she said sharply, "This is addressed to Sara Moone, honey bun. That you?"

"Yes," I croaked in a voice not unworthy of Mrs. K. at her sickliest. Talking to strangers makes me sound like a doormat.

"Oh yes, you're the new one up there at Huddlestons'." She started nodding her head at me, examining me, her mouth grim, her eyes studious slits. "I expect you'll be a handful, with hair on you like that." She put a hand up to her own grizzled head, and seconds before I leapt over the counter to choke the living breath right out of her, she added, "Give my eye-teeth for hair like that." She smiled at me, picked up the other packages, and took them into a room behind the counter. I looked at my hair in the mirror. Dark brown. Reddish. Big deal. Behind me I watched the woman at the table remove her hat, some kind of woollen beret thing. She shoved her fingers under her short hair, fluffing it out. Sandy, faded. She glanced at herself and then her eyes, round, expressionless, met mine.

Quickly, I started zipping up my jacket. I turned up the collar and reached for my package of books. "Wait a minute," the waitress said, appearing again from the back room. "You haven't paid for the kid's Coke."

"Huh?"

"The skinny guy, your whatchamacallit – foster brother?"

"I'm not paying for his Coke." Bye-bye doormat.

All the coffee drinkers were staring at me now. The Elite Cafe was giving daytime TV considerable competition. The door opened, and the boy who had so arrogantly parked himself beside me in the school bus came in. The audience deserted me briefly for him, but came back. Fran said, "The young lad pointed at you when he left, so I figured you were paying."

I started a slow seethe and began to plan Nick's dismemberment. "How much?" Hello sucker.

"Dollar twenty."

I started looking in my pockets for money. I unzipped my jacket and found a penny and a button in the inside pocket. I shoved my hand down into my jeans pocket and fished out two dollars. While I was waiting for the waitress to give me my change, the woman at the table put on her hat and left, followed by the boy, who carried her suitcase. On his way out he looked over at me, surprised, I guess, to see me there. He smiled.

Smiling is not one of the things I do well. I looked away until I heard the door close behind him.

"The paying guest'll be a welcome sight over there at Bellingtons', no doubt," Madam Bulgy said, dabbing at her mouth with a paper napkin.

Earflaps said, "Looks like the young lad's home to stay, then. Them foreign schools he was sent to wasn't a particle o' use to him a'tall. He'll have to parlee voo with a pick and shovel now."

"Not that lad, he won't. I expect the mum's got him workin' as a mater dee or something over there at the bed and breakfast." The bulgy woman talking.

"Come again?"

"Bed and breakfast. You know, like a inn or hotel or one of them. Without the beer parlor."

"Never make a go o' that kind o' thing, not around here."

Mrs. Bulgy kept the conversation rolling. "I'm not one to say I told you so, but, by the Lord Harry, I coulda told you years ago them Bellingtons'd be headin' for the poorhouse at the rate Madam Queen drops money like sand through a sifter."

Fran added her two cents worth. "I think they're making a go of it, all right. The son there seems a nice enough lad. Good family, and it shows. Helps out around the place after school. Came in here one day sayin' he'd like to fix their place up a bit, but he don't know the first thing about carpentry. They're lucky to have a payin' guest at this time of year. Mind you, with the King George burnt to the ground, Bellingtons' is just about the only place in town, unless you count that fleabag over the tracks." She handed me the package.

I flipped up my jacket collar, took the books, and left. At least they can't make a riches-to-rags soap opera about my life. Good family and it shows! Does it show if you have no family? I have that Bellington guy typed. Snob with a capital S.

The change in atmosphere was a shocker after the steamy warmth of the cafe. Outside, the drab sky hung over stale, soot-flecked snow piled around the edges of the parking lot. I looked around for my bike (the Huddlestons' bike, to be accurate). It was no longer propped between the wall and a snowbank. Nothing there but a yellow dog stain. I might have known. If Nick wants something, he takes it. Well, so what? I've walked a few highways in my life.

"Took you long enough," she said when I came in, my face all red and half frozen from walking into the March wind. Ma seems to be short on pleasantries but long on words. She was trotting between fridge and counter, counter and kitchen table, laying out the noon meal. The counter is, in fact, only a vinyl covered board she places over the dish washer and washing machine, lined up beside each other, when they're not in use.

What Ma does by way of passing the time of day is communicate every thought that flits through her head. "Eat some of that baloney for your lunch for I'm not putting it back in the fridge another day 'cause it should've got eat up yesterday but nobody took any notice and I'm not throwing it out sure there's starving children all over the world'd give their right arm for a thick slab o' that but save enough for Hud when he comes in and if there's any of it left we'll have it for supper too for it's waste not want not I always say and a body has to keep up his strength or they'll fall down in a dead faint which is what'll happen to Hud if he don't get on in here out of that blistering wind and him gettin' so short o' breath half the time you'd think he'd be glad of the chance to. Oh. A letter came for you." She picked it up from the kitchen counter and handed it to me.

It was from Ruth, the social worker. There can't be much going on in her life. This is the second time she's written to me.

Outside you could hear Hud, my so-called foster father, hammering at the back, where he was putting on an addition to the little brick box they call a house. It reminds me of a house in a cartoon. When we're all inside I imagine the walls moving in and out like lungs, and when Josh runs around hollering at Nick to give him back his catalog (the kid reads catalogs), I expect the roof to rise up and then come shuddering down.

The day I arrived, Hud had explained, "Want to open her up a bit. Let some air in."

And not before it's time, I'd thought.

"Doin' it all myself."

Wow. Alert the media. Dutifully, I'd looked at the framework of beams and studs he'd put up and said, "Who cares?" I don't expect he heard me.

I hung up my jacket and sat down at the table, put the unopened letter in front of me, and slid my package under the chair. I buttered a piece of bread, letting Ma Huddleston's words wash over me. I'm pretty quiet anyway. I figure if you don't have anything to say, don't flap your lips. But even if I had a burning passion for long chitchats, I'd be out of luck. You can't get a word in edgeways living with Ma Huddleston. I bet I haven't said more than three dozen words since I got here. It doesn't bother me. I mean, I think things; I just don't always blurt them out. The danger with keeping all your thoughts to yourself is that they tend to disappear, like everything else in my life. I guess that's why I keep filing them away in this machine. Nobody can see them except me. They never get out into the world because I don't have a printer. Just me and the machine. I have this feeling that my computer is safe enough to hold even my unborn thoughts. I can also laugh into this thing, laugh at myself and laugh at my colorless, odorless, soundless, nonexistent life. With a computer you don't need a voice.

Anyway, I was still sitting at the table and Ma was still nattering away. "I never saw the beat of you, like talking to a brick wall sure you could be deaf as a post like the young lad we had here Jamie his name was and as nice a lad as ever stood in the sun and oh I used to talk to him not like some that'd act like no hearing meant no brains and he understood every word I . . ." That is a random sample of how she goes on.

I stopped listening to her and started reading Ruth's letter. It was long, about four pages, both sides. Her writing is all slanted to the right, as if she's in a rush to tell you something and can't get it down fast enough. It was full of the same meaningless, who-gives-a-damn questions as the last one. How are you? How's school? How are you getting along with your new family? Are you happy? She ended the last one with "Drop me a line." So I did. In the middle of a piece of paper I dropped: "Dear Ruth, Define happy. Yours with undying respect, Sara Moone."

On the last page of the letter she said: "I know you say you're not interested in making contact with your mother, and I know you know you are under no legal obligation to acknowledge her if she claims you, but in view of the fact that you have had such an unfortunate and unsettled life, and because you appear to me to be desperately unhappy, don't you think it might be in your own best interests to consider settling into a life with someone who obviously wants her daughter back? I have no business interfering in this. There are proper channels through the provincial government, etc., and if you wanted to proceed, everything would be done on the up-and-up – investigations, counseling for both parties, all that sort of thing. But I know this woman doesn't want to wait. Why don't you tell me how you feel about this? In the past you have just clammed up or changed the subject. Are you afraid? Or shy? Or interested but too stubborn to admit it? Just let me know how you feel, and I'll stand by you no matter what."

Good old Ruth. On the right track, but just one step behind. She doesn't know about the clipping. I made a discovery in the reading room at the library one lonely weekend back in the bad old days at Mrs. K.'s. In the classified section of *The Globe and Mail* I happened to see an ad put in by a woman wishing to contact her daughter, born on my exact birth date and given up for adoption soon after. A post office box where the woman could be reached was included. The box number, the city, and the postal code are seared into my memory like a brand.

Here is the reason I refuse to be curious. My birth was the black event that placed me here, in this life, on this road to nowhere. Oh sure, there have been ups and downs and twists and turns, but that's why I can barely remember what my life was like before I was ten or eleven. It changed on such a regular basis that I have nothing to pin it to. Then, by thirteen, life at the Koscyzstins' seemed the exact opposite, one endless stretch of passed gas and darkened rooms.

At the moment, the end of the road leads into a patch of dense gray fog. If I can get through it to sixteen, if I can get far enough along to find a part-time job so I can start heading up north, everything will be pure white, bright and light.

I tore out that ad because it seemed to be a warning – Danger! Thin ice! I don't want to fall through into the black hole. In art class at school I made a black envelope shaped like a twisted, shredded heart and in paint the color of blood I wrote on it "TOO LATE." I stuffed the clipping into the heart envelope and buried the thing in a drawer.

Sitting at Ma Huddleston's kitchen table, I folded Ruth's letter up small, tilted back, and crammed it into the pocket of my jeans. I'll write back to Ruth and say: "Dear

Ruth, I prefer to remain a stray. Stop trying to fit me into the herd. With eternal gratitude, S. M." I will never tell her about the ad in the bottom of my drawer.

I was putting some of Ma's godawful bologna on the slice of buttered, not-bad homemade bread, slathering on some mustard, and folding the bread over, when I was attacked.

"Gimme that!" Josh, Ma's youngest foster darling, put down the barn cat he'd been lugging around, scrambled under the table, and tried to nab my package. I put my foot on it. "Gimme!" he ordered.

I yelled back, "Quit it!" I ducked under the table and bustled the books out of his reach. The cat scampered away to safety.

"Mine!" Josh insisted. He placed his fists on both sides of his eyes and wagged his index fingers like feelers at me.

"What do you think you're doing?"

"Casting a spell. Gimme."

"Here, have this instead, you little blister." Ma Huddleston jammed a sticky bun into Josh's fat little gob. It did the trick. "Books, is it?" Ma aimed a buttery knife at my package. "They got hundreds of books in there at the Ambrose Public Library more than any ten people'd ever read in a month o' Sundays sure you don't need to send away for them to have sumpin' to read."

Ma actually stopped talking, so I changed the subject. "I've been thinking I'd like to look for a part-time job for after school and on weekends. Know of any place where I might get in?"

"A part-time job now why I bet you could try out there at the highway at Fran's Ee-lite, sure I mind the time Fran and me we both got jobs in town down there at Kate's Kozy Kitchen oh it was years ago now mind you and in those days they liked you to wear a uniform which didn't bother me in the least sure it saves the wear and tear on your own duds I tell you they handed them out right left and center, soon as you wore one they'd have it off your back and another one on faster 'n spit, course this was before I married Hud and he come in there one day and he sees me and he says to me . . ."

At this point in Ma's narrative, Hud came in for his noonday meal. It never seems to bother Ma to stop in midsentence. It wasn't a full stop anyway, so much as a right turn. "Sweetie," she said to sticky Josh, "go out to the barn and get that Nick in here right smart or there'll not be a scrap or crumb left for him even though I told him ten minutes ago to get in here but does he ever listen to a word I say no and take that cat out with you aren't we stuffed like sardines in here enough as it is sit down and start Hud and don't stand on ceremony you're half dead-lookin'. Thank God," she prayed briefly over the food. "You want the ketchup?"

"Yep."

CHAPTER

3

I'm about to close down for the night. I know they can hear me tap-tap-tapping after they've all gone to bed. You can hear everything in this place. Once I heard Ma say to Hud something about telling me to turn my machine off because I should be getting more sleep. All he said was, "Leave her be. Needs to talk to the machine more than she needs to sleep." Funny he'd say that. How does he know? Then I heard *creak-sproing* as he rolled over in bed, and ten seconds later he was snoring.

This is a strange house. Not only do I think the walls breathe, but sometimes when I wake up in the middle of the night I sense a throbbing sound with a regular sort of beat. Furnace probably. Or a loud clock.

I've been thinking about that guy who always sits beside me on the school bus and the fact that he came into the Ee-lite and took the paying guest woman to his mother's bed and breakfast. I still think he's a jerk.

I've been thinking about Josh, too. He's a royal pain in the butt. Ma told me he has a mother somewhere who doesn't particularly want him. My sympathies lie with the mother. She might put him up for adoption. At the moment, he's a temporary ward of the Children's Aid. Nobody can adopt him until she bows out and he becomes a Crown ward, like me. I can't imagine anyone crazy enough to adopt the little sucker with his fat legs and runny nose. She should have given him up when he was a baby, before anyone could see how he'd turn out. The other one, Nick, should have been drowned at birth. Totally maladjusted. And not only that, he smells funny. Maybe I have an overly sensitive nose, but I think I can sometimes detect his whereabouts, and the disturbing thing about that is that occasionally I get a whiff of him when I come into my room. Ever since I caught him about to pocket that woman's twenty he's looked as though he's plotting my untimely death. This place wouldn't be half bad if it weren't for all these dysfunctional foster children.

March came in like a lion and now it's going out like a raging bull. So much for old wives' tales. This has been one of the most disgusting days of my life so far. The sheep keep having lambs. I suppose that's what goes on on a farm, but you never think about the actual event. At least I never have. The snow had nearly all disappeared and we were beginning to get a few almost warm days. Mud everywhere. Dog dirt thawing in puddles. Picturesque as all hell. Went to bed one night to the tune of raindrops and a howling wind and woke up before daylight to knee-high snow and Ma hauling us all out of our beds to help Hud with the new lambs. Two were sick or something and had to be wrapped in blankets and carried through this howling blizzard into the kitchen. A ewe died and its lamb had to be fed with a bottle. All this stuff. I've read about things like this, but I never thought I'd be involved. I mean up to my ankles in actual sheep shit – smell of wet crap-covered wool getting warm and drying – and the way the lamb nearly pulled the bottle out of my hand sucking like mad. You could tell it was a life-and-death thing. Sticky milk dribbling out of its mouth, finally.

I'm not saying it was exciting or made me feel good or anything. I'm just saying it was a wrinkle in my otherwise flat existence. Everybody was in on the act. Josh, of course, was underfoot the whole time saying, "My turn. Gimme. Lemme do it." Finally, I said, "Okay, do it," and let him hold the bottle. The way he looked at me you'd think I'd handed him the keys to the Buick. Biggest mistake I ever made. He kept hanging around me, sitting beside me, staring up at me with these glistening eyes he has. I hate that kind of thing.

Nick was next to useless. He yelled at Hud about the dead ewe, insisting that it wasn't really dead and why didn't he lift it up and help it and all that. Ma grabbed him and tried to drag him away from the dead animal, but he punched Ma in the chest. He hurt her, too, I could tell, but she just kept right on trying to hug him and calm him down until finally Hud roared at him and he went into the house. I don't know what his particular problem is.

Even the stupid dog wanted part of the action. It followed us right into the house when we were bringing the lambs in. Ma turned on the oven and opened the oven door for added heat, and the dog stretched out with its head on its paws close to where we had placed the lambs. I thought Ma would shoo it back outside, but she didn't. She didn't even go into a one-way conversation, an event in itself. She looked at me and shrugged and went down to the cellar to see if she could find some old curtain to wrap around the lambs. When they started to come around and make little lamb sounds, something halfway between a meow and a bleat, the dog lifted up its head and said – Oh, this sounds stupid. It made some kind of a dog sound, like yip or something. But it sounded – at the time – like "Yep." I mean the dog always hangs around Hud, and I know I'm imagining it, but it did sound – a little bit – like, well, yep. Okay, so I'm crazy. Not too surprising considering where I live.

The school bus was canceled because of the blizzard. Everything was more or less under control by about noon. Hud had rigged up a warm nest for the lambs in the barn and Ma and I were drinking coffee after cleaning up the kitchen. I was just sitting there at the table gazing at the snapshots she has pinned to every square inch of wall space – former foster kids, I guess. One or two grown up now – a bride, a guy in a Mountie uniform. There were kids with twisted arms and legs, fat kids, tall kids, and quite a few babies, the snapshots faded and curling. I was listening to Ma blather on about the weatherman and his role in the present unseasonal situation. Josh was studying the Canadian Tire catalog as if he had to write an exam on it. Nick came into the kitchen and said in a kind of frightened, breathless way, "Look at Edith-Ann." Josh and Ma both peered down at the dog sitting beside me. It had put its head under my hand, and without even thinking, I sort of let my fingers massage the back of its head behind the ears. I looked down, too, and there was this animal, this beast, sitting there baring its teeth, seconds away from removing my hand at the wrist and devouring it. For a fraction of a second I froze, not knowing quite what to do. I stopped patting it. I could hear this low growl coming from the back of its throat.

Ma bellowed at it, "Edith-Ann! Kitchen!" And it slunk away over near the door.

It hates me. This mongrel hates my living guts. What did I ever do to it? Why should I feel so shattered? Why did Ma order it to the kitchen? It was already there.

All I could think of to say was, "Edith-Ann! How could you give this monster a name like Edith-Ann?"

"Josh named her when she arrived in our backyard last summer," Ma said. "Our own dog, the one we'd had for oh I don't know how many years he was an awful good dog but so lame finally he couldn't stand up and poor Hud felt so bad course he had to be –"

I looked at Josh. "Edith-Ann?"

"You got a problem with that?"

I kind of turned my palms up to the ceiling. It doesn't

matter to me what they call the stupid thing. "Sandy," I said, "Trixie. Only kind of dog's names I've ever heard of. Never heard of one called Edith-Ann."

Ma said, "Josh named her after someone he remembers who was kind to him once and why not I'd like to know for it's little enough loving-kindness goes on in this world for some unlucky kids so why not make the most of it and keep a little kindness close to hand while you can."

Ma only paused for breath, but I jumped in. "But the dog's vicious. Why would you want to keep a –" I didn't get a chance to finish because Hud came in.

He said, "Give her a chance. She's a stray. God only knows what she's had to put up with. She may come around."

"Oh, sure," I said.

Hud leaned against the door jamb while he eased off his rubber boots in the little mud room attached to the kitchen. "She hasn't bit anybody yet."

I looked at my hand. "I sure don't plan to be the first."

Hud looked at the ceiling and said in this quiet voice as if he was forcing himself to be patient, "We all gotta try to get along."

What a day! After the save-the-sheep episode and the mad-dog ordeal I felt like barricading myself in my room and communing with my machine, which I quite happily did for the best part of the afternoon. I had just finished quoting Hud's immortal sentiment, "We all gotta try to get along," when somebody tried to break down my door.

Josh. "Lemme in!" he screeched.

"Go away," I said. "You're a pain in the rear end."

"Oping! I need you." He kicked the door, then set up a howl.

I lifted the hook, my only protection from invaders, opened the door a crack, and peered out.

"Now see what you did? Breaked m' foot!" Josh growled. He took advantage of the slightly opened door to poke his hand through and grab the bottom of my sweatshirt. The cat he had been carting around jumped out of his arms and scooted down the stairs.

I yelled at him to let go.

"Make me." He squinted up his eyes trying to look tough, but failed. He has the misfortune to have those big dark eyes they paint on velvet to show some smarmy, tear-jerking toddler.

I tried to pry his fingers loose with one hand while holding the door with the other, but it was too awkward. A strong kid, Josh. I let the door swing wide and he catapulted right into my stomach. Then he made a beeline for my bed, landing squarely in the middle.

I said, "You have two seconds to get out. One, two."

"Read me a story."

"No."

"Why not?"

"I'm busy."

"Y'are not. Tell me one, then."

"I don't know any. Now go away."

"Do so."

I narrowed my eyes at Josh. O evil, evil. "All right," I said. "I'll tell you a little story." I smoothed my lips across the front of my face, imitating a smile, tore off my headband, and pushed my fingers up through my hair to give it – shall we say – character. Josh seemed to shrink away as if I were a witch, but I sat beside him on the bed and beamed him another lippy smile. Smile enough for Josh, I guess. He wriggled himself up close to me into a story-listening position. Any closer and he'd have been sitting on me.

"Are you ready for this?" I asked.

He nodded.

I sincerely doubted it. I began. "Adam and Eve and Pinch-Me went down to the river to bathe." Josh's eyes were limpid pools of eagerness. I continued, "Adam and Eve fell in, and who do you think was saved?" I looked at Josh.

"What?"

"Adam and Eve fell in and who was saved?"

"Who?"

"You're supposed to say Pinch-Me, stupid."

"Pinch me!" Josh yelled obligingly. "Ow!" he shrieked when I pinched him. He let his mouth hang open and stared at me. He couldn't believe it. He shoved up his sleeve, twisted his arm around, and looked at the red spot I'd left.

His lower lip trembled, but he didn't cry. He blinked several times, looking up into my eyes. I tried to make my own eyes round and empty, the way I always do, but I wasn't succeeding. I blinked once or twice, too, but all I could see was this hurt look on his face. It was ridiculous. I'd pinched him pretty hard, but not that hard. No blood. No broken bones.

I just kept seeing something shattered around the chocolate-drop eyes. I wanted to laugh at him. I wanted him to run away so that I could laugh him right out of my life, but he didn't run away. And I couldn't make myself laugh. I felt – ooo, I hate to say this – I felt sheepish. Sheepish? Forget sheepish. I felt as if I'd pulled the dirtiest trick in the book, like slaughtering Santa Claus.

"Suppertime!" Ma bellowed from downstairs.

I stood up and Josh squirmed off my bed onto the floor. He stood there looking down at his bottom lip with his shoulders drooping. All right, so I shouldn't have done it. He's just a little kid. Big deal. This is what life's all about. Get somebody first before they get you. It's something he has to learn.

Then I started thinking, maybe he's a slow learner. Hard to explain why, but I reached down and put my hand on his shoulder. "Go ahead and tell on me, if you want," I said.

He sidled out from under my hand and stumped off down the stairs without a word.

Neither Josh nor I said anything during supper, not that we were given a chance with Ma highlighting her afternoon's events for the entertainment of all present. Slick Nick managed to get in a request for seconds while Ma was in midbite and before she got nicely launched into a long-winded description of the talk show she'd been watching before supper. Ma says she hates talk shows.

Josh sat across from me. Every once in a while he looked up and over at me. His eyes kept haunting me across his spaghetti, which he wasn't eating, not even after Hud cut it up for him.

Even though I kept telling myself, this is not a big deal, I was having trouble swallowing. Spaghetti is the one thing that makes my mouth water, especially the way Ma cooks it, but I could hardly get it down. I sat there winding and rewinding it on my fork. So I pinched him. He deserved it. He's a royal pain. Every time I looked up, there was Josh looking at me like a slapped puppy. He told Ma he didn't want dessert and left the table.

It was Nick's turn to help clear up the dishes. He started taking them away one at a time, dragging his way across to the sink as if it was a major hardship. "Go on," I said, "I'll do it." I couldn't stand watching him and I couldn't stand thinking about Josh. Mainly, I couldn't stand myself.

They *all* stared at me now. Ma put a thoughtful finger on her buttoned lip. Hud cleared his throat, looked at Josh's empty chair and then back at me. "Mm-hmm," he said and left the table.

I loaded the dishwasher, and Ma said she'd do the pots.

When the work was finished, I decided to take a little stroll through the house. Stroll! Five easy steps and you've had the tour. I creaked up the narrow stairs and glanced into the bedrooms. The Huddlestons' sagging bed, the boys' rat's nest, and my own tidy cubbyhole, Sugar 'n Spice still turned to the wall, were all that I saw. No Josh, although I wasn't really looking for him. Downstairs in the living room Nick and Hud were watching TV, slouched back on the leatherette couch. Ma was yakking on the phone in the kitchen, tilted forward on a wooden stool, her elbows propped on the washing machine.

I put on my coat and boots and went out. It wasn't very cold. It had stopped snowing ages ago and was dark now except for the yard light that lit up the path we'd trampled in the snow going to and from the barn. Not even the dog had disturbed the fresh snow on either side of the path. All the old brown melting muck was covered over with a white blanket as if spring were being given a second chance to get it right.

In front of me the barn loomed. The light in the hay mow was on and the small door cut into its wider one hung open. Through it I could see Josh under the light-bulb, sitting cross-legged on the floor. So big miraculous deal! I could turn around and go back to the house. Under the hay room I could hear the sheep make a low bleating sound as I turned to go back. Muffled by the snow, it sounded like *boo-o-o-o!*

I stopped because I felt myself freezing up. I had to look back through the barn door while I could still move my head. Josh's head was bent over his crossed rubber boots. His back in it's too-small sweater was curved, exposing his pale neck to the night, except where little curls of baby hair protected it.

A barn cat pounced at my feet and ran into the shadows, and I found I could move. I walked toward the glare of the lightbulb.

It was warm in the barn. Loose straw littered the floor and bales of hay were piled at the far end. Near one wall Edith-Ann lay in a straw nest with her chin on her paws. She raised her head when I came in. In the middle of the barn, on the floor, Josh picked at bits of straw.

"Hey Josh!"

Silence.

"Josh?" He wouldn't look at me, so I said, "Listen, you can do it to me if you want; you can get me back. Say, Adam and Eve and Pinch-Me . . ."

He shook his head. He was picking up pieces of straw and trying to fit one inside the hollow end of another. When it didn't work, he broke them. I stood watching him. One of the cats rubbed up against his shoulder, but he paid no attention to it. I crouched down.

"Go ahead and pinch me." I shucked off my coat, shoved up my sleeve, and stuck my bare arm under his nose, but he shifted away from me.

"Bite it, then, or give it a punch."

"You're sick."

I squatted there and stared at him and thought, he's right, the little sucker. I sat down on the floor near him, picking at the straw. I managed to fit one inside another and showed him, but he turned away. "Okay, look," I said at last. "Here's what you say if someone tries Adam and Eve and Pinch-Me on you again."

He turned toward me with his head down but finally let his eyes tilt up. It was a this-is-your-last-chance kind of look.

I said, "When they say, 'and who do you think was saved?' you say, 'Pinch me not.'"

Josh's face was a blank. "It means, don't pinch me. See? That's how you can fool them. Nobody can ever trick you again, not even me, because you know a better answer. Just say, 'Pinch me not.'"

Warily, he tried it out. "Pinch me not." He edged a little away, but nothing happened. He smiled. "Pinch me not," he said again and laughed. Edith-Ann's tail thumped in the straw.

He scrambled to his feet and headed for the house. I put my jacket back on and followed behind him along the narrow snow-path, glittering now, strewn with diamonds. The sheep were still putting in their two cents worth. "*A-a-ah*," they were bleating.

In the living room Nick was deeply involved in "Star Trek." "Pinch me not," Josh yelled at him. "Star Trek" must have beamed Nick up and out of the normal world, because nothing happened. "Oh boy," Josh whispered as I came into the room, "I think you maked me invisible. Oh boy." He put his fingers near his eyes, wagged them, and whispered slowly, magically, "P-inch m-ee n-ot-t."

I'm back up in my room clicking all this into my machine. I would feel forgiven if I actually cared about the stupid little jerk.

I need some fast money so I can escape. That part-time

job Ma and I talked about, that's what I need. This place is beginning to get under my skin. When I came into my room just now, I had the feeling someone's been in here shifting my stuff around. The little bit of money I have is still well hidden. It would take a genius to find it. I'm not even revealing its hiding place to this machine.

I wonder why I even did Adam and Eve and Pinch-Me on him. Forget it. Of course, somebody did it to me once, ages ago. You'd think I'd have forgotten about it. What made me dredge it up?

When I first got this computer, I took the back off to see what was in there, what made it remember things. All I saw was something that looked like miniature Lego pieces interlocked in an important way. It didn't give up any secrets.

Sometimes, like right now, when I think about my own past, my early life seems to be a series of small dark caves, each with its own secret scrabblings, its unexpected flutterings. I hate that. In each cave there are bottomless swirling black holes. I have to stop doing this. I have to stop thinking in case I get sucked in, down, flushed away into another time, over which I have no control. As long as I think into this machine, I have control.

It's safe to examine my present through a machine.

There's nothing wrong with Adam and Eve and Pinch-Me. Josh is too young to get it, that's all. Funny I didn't know that. Am I a bully? This machine is smart, but not smart enough to answer that.

CHAPTER

4

The snow is nearly all gone, except where it's drifted into shaded places behind the henhouse and under the scrub cedars along one side of the road. Ever since Easter we've had a stretch of sunny days drying things up so you can walk out the kitchen door without squelching through mud lake.

On the way home from school yesterday I got off the school bus at the Ee-lite. I decided I might as well start asking around about jobs. That Bellington guy got off, too. It's his stop. A few kids started yelling smart-ass things when I followed him off the bus, Nick included. Cheers and whistles and everything. "Way t'go Matt!" some jerk yelled.

I imagined myself inside a tinted-glass, soundproof box and didn't hear anything after that. I didn't even hear him come into the cafe behind me. His name is Matthew Bellington. Classy, or what?

I sat at the far end of the counter. There were only two other people at the counter, the bulgy woman and a bulgier woman. They were talking about how badly we needed rain and how warm the sun was for the time of year. Fran, the waitress, was deeply into the discussion but finally tore herself away long enough to come down to my end of the counter.

"Get you something?" she asked.

I started stuttering over my words the way I usually do when I talk to strangers, especially in public. "I want to get a part-time job," I blurted. "I was wondering if you needed –" I stopped because Matthew Bellington sat down on the stool next to mine.

Fran said, "Are you kidding? We'd be tripping over each other. Maybe I could use the help sometimes, but I don't have the space. This is a one-woman operation. Sorry."

"That's okay."

"You want a Coke or anything?"

I shook my head and got up to go, but Matthew put his hand on the sleeve of my jacket and said, "Wait."

I jumped about a foot and yanked my arm away. His mouth fell open and his face turned red. He took his glasses off and started to apologize, but I said I had to get home. He put his glasses back on. I half turned to go, but I couldn't get my legs to move. It might have had something to do with the way he had just looked at me – as if he had been clumsy and had accidentally broken a valuable piece of crystal.

Fran interrupted at that moment. "Listen, honey bun," she said. "Come to think of it, I wouldn't mind sleeping in Saturdays. You come in this Saturday and I'll show you where things are, what to do. We'll see how it works out."

I nodded. I got my legs moving and opened the door. I sensed Matthew Bellington right behind me. Instead of shoving through the door and letting it go, never mind the guy behind, I held it, waited till he caught it. I'm going to the dogs.

He said, "Thanks."

I said zip.

He said, "Sorry I frightened you."

I hate people who apologize. I puffed air out through the corner of my mouth. I walked across the parking lot, but he stayed beside me.

"I just wanted to tell you that someone I know asked me if I knew anyone who wanted a part-time job. That's all. Too late, though, I guess."

"Doing what?" I stopped at the edge of the road.

He stopped, too. "Typing."

"In-i-i-in an office?" This could be a little more rewarding, I thought, than Saturday mornings at the Ee-lite Cafe and Bus Terminal.

"No, in your own home. Except that I think you'd need a computer."

"I have a computer."

"Well –"

So, the bottom line is that some old guy named Grainger Cleary books a room at Matt's mother's bed and breakfast every summer, produces a kazillion pages of handwriting, and wants someone to type it. Too bad I don't have a printer.

I thought about that kind of job, though, all the way back to the Huddlestons'. Reading somebody else's writing. A book, maybe. He must be a writer. Helping some guy produce an actual book. I think I've heard of him – Grainger Cleary.

The sun was just about level with my eyes going up the last hill before home. I mean the Huddlestons'. I could hear Hud hammering, working on his addition. I shaded my eyes with my hand and pretty soon the square box of a house came into view, perched on top of the hill. Hud's new room was beginning to take shape. You could tell where the windows would be. Nearly all windows it seemed. It flared out from the rest of the house as if it would set sail. And Hud up there standing astride the peak, waving. Break his neck if he fell off. Thinks he's bloody captain of the thing. He must have thought I was waving at him the way I had my hand up blocking the sun. Cripes. So I waved back. I hate that so much.

What did I ever do to deserve the role of bodyguard for Josh? You'd think I could have five minutes alone to commune with my computer, but no. Crash, bang, pound my door to sawdust. He's strong enough, you'd think he could fight his own battles.

I rolled back the last few paragraphs I'd written and squinted hard at my monitor screen, ignoring him, but he whammed the door relentlessly, rhythmically. "Beat it, Josh," I hollered, "and I mean it."

"I need you. Nickie hit me!" he wailed.

I pressed save and exit and turned the thing off. I scraped my chair back and unhooked the door. "This better be serious," I said. I glowered down at him from my full height, but he refused to shrivel away.

Cradling one arm in the other, he turned up his tear-streaked, pudding-pot face. "Nickie breaked m'arm," he sniffed.

"Well, don't tell me about it. Go tell Ma."

"She can't listen at me. I need *you*." His eyes blinked a hopeful S.O.S. at me.

I know what he means about Ma. Ma loves Josh to pieces and spoils him beyond hope, but it's hard to get her attention once she's got her mouth in motion. It's like going downhill with no brakes.

"Oh, all right." I let out a long sucker-of-the-year sigh. "Let me look at it." Josh displayed a scraped and bruised forearm that made me bite my lip. I checked the upper part of his bad-luck arm. The pinch mark I'd made seemed to have disappeared. He was still looking up at me as if I possessed X-ray vision and a cape.

"Why did Nickie do this?" I asked.

"Because."

"Why because?"

Josh studied his banged-up arm. "Because I said Ma is so my real mother. And Nickie, he said no she's not. He said my real mother's coming to get me one of these days. He said, 'She's gonna get you.' So I spit on his foot." He looked up at me. "Don't let her."

"You spit on his foot?"

"His bare foot. A big glob."

"That's disgusting!"

"Well, don't let him say that, then. Don't let my mother get me."

I shrugged. "I can't stop her. I'm not magic."

"He didn't need to break m'arm, did he?"

"No, he didn't. He's a bully and bullies are something I can deal with." Lo and behold! The avenging angel!

I set off in search of Nick, Josh trailing behind, sniffling hard. He wasn't in his room where Josh had left him and he wasn't watching TV with Ma and her neighbor Mrs. Oaksi.

I figured he'd put on his shoes and gone outside. The days are longer now. It stays light after supper.

We found him behind the barn tying pieces of binder twine into one long rope. "Listen, buster," I said, "next time you feel like bullying someone, pick on somebody your own size." I nearly gagged at the sound of my voice.

Nick stuffed the twine into his pocket and slouched, arms folded, against the barn wall. "I didn't do nothin'."

I can't stand this guy. For one thing, his hair always looks stringy. Ma makes him shower every day, but maybe nobody ever told him hair-washing is part of the deal. Maybe that's why he smells. And I can't stand the way his eyes slide around, roving up and down my body as if he's trying to see if there are any gaps in my clothes. I moved a little behind Josh. I even put my hand on his shoulder, as if that would do any good.

"Did so," piped up Josh. "Breaked m'arm with a big stick."

"You didn't have to hit him." I glared at Nick.

There was a long pause while his eyes slid from me to Josh and back to me. He stared at my hand on Josh's shoulder. He straightened away from the barn wall, puffing out his chest, trying to fill out his lean frame. "He bugs me. Gets away with murder 'cause he's Ma's little pet."

"I don't see you suffering any. Any other home would have kicked you out long ago. You're a troublemaker."

"Don't worry, I'll be out of here soon enough. My mother's looking for a new place to live. Soon as she gets it, I'm moving back in with her."

"In a pig's eye," I said. "I've heard that one so many times it's stale."

"What?"

"Nothing."

"I'm never leaving here," Josh said. "And nobody can make me, 'cause I'm invisible."

Losers, the two of them.

"Invisible, right," Nick snorted. "Come here, sweetheart. I'll make you invisible."

"Leave him alone!" I stood in front of Josh now. "Don't touch him again. Ever." I didn't stammer at all. My voice was like the edge of a razor blade. Nick stood there, smiling. He knows how to make his eyes look as though they've just violated you.

Even Josh seemed to notice. He got around in front of me again and said, "So there."

Nick belted out this sharp laugh he has. "Do you think you can actually stop me?"

I said, "Your mother doesn't even know you exist. And if she did, she'd abandon you all over again."

Nick laughed again, a dry, whistling sound between barely parted, unsmiling lips. He said, "Does yours?"

I wasn't sure I'd heard him right. "What did you say?" I asked him, my heart pounding.

He whinnied another laugh that lasted longer than was absolutely necessary. "I *said*," he said, "did you know Josh is accident prone? He's always getting hurt and there doesn't seem to be anything he can do about it."

"Mothers don't come back for kids like you," I said. "She's out there with a beautiful place of her own and some man she lives with, and her other kids, nice kids, not like you. She's glad to be rid of you. Lucky to be rid of you."

Nick's cheeks and mouth stiffened. He took his eyes away from my body. They looked unfocused, as if he saw something we couldn't, something just behind us, or beside us. I saw his jaw muscles bulge and slacken a couple of times as he clenched his teeth. He took the rope out of his pocket and fiddled with it, tying knots, not saying anything, thinking. He sighed then and his bluster seemed to sag with his shoulders. When he spoke, he sounded like someone reading out loud. "I realize it was a very bad thing to do."

I couldn't believe this guy. I think my mouth was hanging open. "What did you just say?" I asked him.

He looked straight into my shocked face and said, "I'm sorry I did it. Sorry I hurt Josh." His pale green eyes were wide and clear as glass and a sudden smile appeared, curving up like a happy-face drawing. "Hey, pal," he said to Josh. "I didn't mean to. I take it back, okay?"

"Okay," sniffed Josh.

Nickie waved the rope at us and walked away twirling it in the air.

I'm not absolutely sure about this, but the end of that rope looked an awful lot like a noose. "Let's go," I said to Josh.

"Wait!" he said. He was examining his arm and sniffing with all his might.

"Come on, forget about it."

"It's still broke!" he wailed. His tears started again and his nose was a mess.

"Let Ma deal with it then." I marched him back to the house to be presented to Ma, who was easily located by the sound of her never-ending voice.

". . . and I never in all my born days saw anything the beak of it as big as a turkey almost and twice as ugly but I never meant to sideswipe it though sideswipe it I did and bent the fender and that musta been on the Tuesday 'cause Hud was gone to town in the truck, it was when we had the Pontiac that time the fella down the road said it'd never run a month and sure it never stopped till the day I . . ."

"MA!" I interrupted Ma's evening monologue. Mrs. Oaksi sat in the swivel rocker the Huddlestons have in their living room, which made it easy for her to nod knowingly in Ma's direction one minute and chuckle at the sitcom on TV the next. Apparently Mrs. Oaksi speaks very little English. Ma, it seems, is doing her level best to make her learn, in large quantity and at high volume.

I had Ma's attention. "Look at Josh's arm. He got hit with a stick," I explained without exactly telling on Nick. Having something to snitch about is like having something in a bank account. You save it till you need it.

Ma pulled Josh, wincing, close to her and examined the injury. Mrs. Oaksi looked, too, tut-tutting and shaking her head.

"And if you see a pinch mark," I added, self-righteously, I have to admit, "I did it." There now. Washed clean.

Ma looked at me with raised eyebrows but didn't comment. "Does she bend?" she asked Josh indicating his arm.

Josh obliged by bending and straightening it.

"Well, you'll live to see another day or two I expect and one of these days you'll learn to keep away from bad lads and not lay yourself open to gettin' beat up on like it's one of the facts of life you're going to have to learn the hard way, not like most kids I've had around here know when to keep their mouth shut and steer clear of the riffraff like those unwashed kids down by the tracks but you'll catch on sooner or later, which one of them hit you?"

"Nickie."

"Nickie! Oh! Well! Dear me! But I s'pose I might have known it'd be Nick for I've seen it coming on this last year though he tries so hard to be good just to please me I sometimes think but it's like he was born on a one-way street heading ass-backward all the way but I'll have a word with him don't you fear and you'll just have to learn to keep an eye in the back of your head 'cause if you don't you'll end up . . ."

I had to break in on this. "Ma! He's only little. How can he figure all that out? It's going to take more than a word with Nick to solve the problem."

Ma pondered this. She put a sympathetic hand on Josh's head and got up out of her chair. "I'm going to get him a Band-Aid," she shouted at Mrs. Oaksi, pointing to Josh's bruised arm. Mrs. Oaksi nodded total agreement.

"Joshy want a Band-Aid?" she crooned.

"Yes," he sniffed, his lower lip quivering again.

"For all the good that'll do," I muttered and escaped back to the relative calm of my own room, where I've got my machine humming again.

I thought I smelled Nick again. However, nothing's missing. Maybe I just have a highly developed imagination – or sense of smell, like a dog, which is a frightening thought. Shades of Edith-Ann.

5

Tomorrow I go in to work at the Ee-lite, absolutely on my own, without Fran there telling me what to do. I know what to do. She's spent the past two Saturdays showing me the ropes, as she says. You don't exactly have to be a genius to figure it out.

Two weeks ago, after Fran said she'd give me the job, I phoned Ruth to tell her about it.

"Congratulations," she said. "That's wonderful!"

"It's not the Nobel Prize. It's only a part-time job."

"But I'm proud of you."

"Good Lord."

"It's good experience."

"Listen, I've got a chance for another job in the summer." I told her about the man who needed a typist. "I'm thinking of maybe getting a printer if I can find one cheap. I could probably make enough money at the Ee-lite to buy one by the time summer rolls around. It would be like an investment. All the money I make I want to put toward getting up north. But if I have a printer, I can probably make even more, so spending it on a printer is not throwing it away. See what I mean?"

"Of course." She went on. "Or you could save it for your education, which would also be an investment in the future. You could go up north after you become something – a teacher, maybe, or a –"

"Ruth, get in touch. I'm dropping out, remember? I have no interest in becoming something."

She wasn't listening. "Or a social worker or even a –"

"Garbage collector." There was a pause at the other end. "Bye, Ruth," I said. "Phone me sometime when you're back on this planet." I hung up.

Next, I decided I should let Ma know where I would be on Saturdays, not that she'd be likely to notice whether I was on site or not. She was in her place of business as she calls it. The kitchen. Nick was there, handy, waiting for his next meal. Josh was hunting for his catalog.

"I've got a Saturday job," I said fast before she could get her mouth open to talk. Ma was engaged in smearing a last dollop of icing on a long slab of chocolate cake.

"That's nice dear sure when I was your age I held down two jobs one in the day and the other at night talk about tired worked off my feet half the time, doing what?" She was going to swoosh hot water into the scraped mixing bowl but changed her mind. She handed it to Nick along with a spoon. He clutched it as if someone might try to take it away from him. He slid his eyes in Josh's direction. Josh had found his catalog and was studying garden tractors.

"Working behind the counter at the –"

"Exactly what I said you should try to get and well I remember workin' myself at Kate's Kozy course I was a good bit older than you by then this was before I married Hud just a year before, I swear when he come in that time and he sees me and he says to me – Get your feet off that table you young blister were you born in a barn or what?" She took a swipe with the dish towel at Nick, who sat tilted back in a chair, licking the bowl, one foot propped against the table edge. He let his chair down with a bang. Something like a threat narrowed his eyes.

Ma tsk-tsked at him and he turned all sweet and innocent looking. "Go on out now and get Hud in here before his supper's dried up to nothing," Ma said.

"Hey," Josh wailed, his attention on the licked icing bowl. "How come – ?"

"Next time," Ma said. "You got the last one, fair's fair, and wash your hands the two of you you're not sitting down to the table with hands on you like that oh you're in already are you?" She noticed Hud.

"Yep," he replied.

That was two weeks ago. I am now an expert at making coffee and tea, grilling hamburgers, and making sandwiches. Fran buys doughnuts and muffins from a bakery, but she makes the hamburger patties herself and also the sandwich fillings. She usually has homemade soup, a different one every three days and a special – beef stew, which is kind of stringy, chicken potpie, which is delicious, or chili, which I can take or leave. I recommend the sandwiches.

The cafe regulars acted as if I had two heads the first time I turned up for work with Fran. I noticed them sizing me up over the rims of their coffee cups. I felt as if I were on stage and didn't know what play I was in. There wasn't any of the usual gabbing back and forth, or arguing about the weather. Fran serves the coffee in mugs with saucers. Every time I picked one up my hand shook so much that the whole room echoed with the sound of rattling cups. I figured out how to use the cash register without any trouble and I can total bills and count out change like a human calculator.

The second Saturday I worked, Hud came in. He sat there on a stool and looked identical to the other old buzzards, except younger. He took off his cap and sat on it for lack of a better place to put it. He had a crease around his head from his hat and his hair stuck out at an angle, but Hud never cares about things like that. Even if he looked in a mirror, he wouldn't notice.

"S'posed t' rain," he said without looking at anybody.

"We can use it," Earflaps said. It was nearly the end of April, but no one had bothered to tell him he wasn't in any danger of freezing his ears off.

I rattled a coffee over to Madam Bulgy and tried to ask Hud what he'd like. First of all I couldn't make my voice work. Then it came out in a loud croak, and I started to stutter.

"Coke," he said, and before I could work up to asking him whether he wanted a large one or a small one, he said, "Small." That made it easy. He smiled at me this way he has of smiling. Calmly. He doesn't have to use any smile muscles. His face seems to fall naturally into it. And his eyes make you imagine he's thinking kind things about you.

What a pile that is! I'll probably backspace it out next time I scroll it up.

Then I went *bing-bing-bing* on the cash register and I heard Fran say, "Smart as a whip the young lady is." I felt myself turning red and tried to pretend I was deaf.

"Oh, she's a right lass, that one," Hud said. Whatever that meant.

"Right as rain," someone said.

"Oh, she's the lass." I think that was Madam Bulgy.

A stranger came in then, which was just as well or they'd have been stuck on the same line till somebody pulled their plugs. He asked for directions to someplace and got about four different versions of how to get there. He looked at me as if I were part of the establishment and asked for coffee. I got it for him. He asked what kinds of sandwiches we had, and I said, "Egg salad, tuna with or without lettuce, and ham on rye or plain."

"Tuna, no lettuce," he said.

"Might rain and it might not," Fran said.

"S'posed to," Hud said.

It wasn't until after Hud left that I realized I had stopped croaking and stuttering and rattling cups.

Matthew Bellington sat beside me on the bus today, again. He doesn't always, but if he doesn't, nobody else does. I thought I had his type figured out, but I keep changing my mind. Snob just doesn't cover it.

Besides me, there are only four other girls on the bus. They appear to come as matched sets, something like salt and pepper, cream and sugar. They think I am, variously: stuck-up, a nerd, an alien, boring. They also believe I'm deaf, I guess.

Their views on Matt are: stuck-up, a nerd, an alien, and good-looking. Also deaf.

Usually I look out the window and pretend I'm standing alone on the snow-swept tundra. When he sits beside me, he always says, "Hi-how-are-you-doing?"

I always answer him, or try to. But I have to clear my throat about three times before I can make the sound come out. So it comes out "*Cark-cark-cark-okay.*" He probably thinks I'm dying of some respiratory disorder. Anyway, today, after the preliminaries, he asked me, "Are you interested in that typing job?"

I dragged myself in off the tundra. "Sure," I whispered, after carking my lungs raw.

He told me that Grainger Cleary, the guy who needs the typist, is coming earlier this year than he had last. "He's coming the twenty-fourth of May long weekend and staying until sometime in August. He pays room and board, so that's good news for my mother and me."

I nodded.

"Now I need a job."

I looked at him, puzzled. I wanted to ask why he hadn't

taken the typing job. I said, "Wh-wh-wh – ?" Fortunately, he interrupted me.

"I've applied for a university scholarship for next fall, but there's no guarantee I'll get it. Anyway, even if I do, it won't cover everything."

"Wh-wh-wh – ?"

"I've tried a few places, building contractors mainly. I want to do something useful. But they want someone with experience." He shifted around with his back against the seat arm, one foot up on the seat, as if he wanted to be able to look at me while he was talking. He took off his glasses and dangled them over his bent up knee. It was just as though we were two people you'd see somewhere on a bus, talking. I mean we *were* two people on a bus, but . . .

This is hard to explain. I felt as if the "I" out on the tundra were watching these two people. It was like watching a medium-good movie. I was kind of interested and forgot to mangle my words. I said, "Why don't you take the typing job?"

"Well, for one thing, I haven't got a computer. I don't even have a typewriter. And for another, I want to learn how to do things. You know? Shingle a roof or hang a door or build steps. I don't want to go down in history as some guy with a university degree but no skills."

"Go down in history?" I had turned in my seat now, my knees up under my chin looking at this guy who might go down in history. I leaned my head back against the window. What a concept! I have always thought of history as chunks of time, eras, something connected to reigns, or wars, or movements. But the way he said that made me think of ordinary people linked together, going back and back and back. Or even forward. Not that he's an ordinary person. He probably will turn up in some future history book. Down at the Ee-lite they say that his family used to be quite rich and he's been away to private school and all that and he's some kind of genius. His father died when he was little, and his mother never got over it. She went off her nut temporarily and spent nearly everything they had. You could write a movie about that. Probably been done.

I remember the conversation down at the cafe. Madam Bulgy started it off, saying, "She asked me last fall did I know anyone would come in and clean."

"Who?" Earflaps asked.

"Mrs. Bellington."

"Cripes." He looked at his neighbors left and right. They shook their heads. "There'd be scant pay in that."

"Why's that?" Mrs. Bulgy's bulgier friend asked. She was apparently an outsider in the gossip department.

"Flat bust."

"Bankrupt?"

"Oh, I don't know about bankrupt, but I'll tell y' – Ever hear tell of blood from a stone?"

"What do you mean?"

"You can't get it."

"Lady B.!" sniffed the bulgy woman. "I heard Lawyer Crestwick wanted a silver teapot for services rendered and our Lady Bellington said he'd get it in the back of his skull was the only way he'd get it. She may have frittered away the family fortune, but I'll guarantee she knows the whereabouts and value of every item in every room of the house right down to the last gold thimble. She's shrewd, by times, that one."

Somebody else chimed in, "Wouldn't you think she'd sell things off, though, with a son to educate and feed and all that? Sure they have to eat." They drank their various beverages, pondering this necessity.

Conversation is communal property in the Ee-lite. Farther down the counter someone said, "It's the end of an era, I tell you, the end of an era. Time was when that family and two or three others up the valley there ruled like lords of the land around here. Made their money years ago, up the river, in timber. Slipped right through their fingers so it did. Slipped right through."

"If the husband was alive today," Fran said, "they'd be back on their feet. He had a head on him. But what can you expect with old John Crestwick managing their affairs? Sure he's been a see-nile old coot all his life and now he's in his dotage, he's that much worse."

Sitting beside me in the school bus, Matt was talking away while I was thinking about the way everybody around here takes a personal interest in everybody else's affairs. They seem to be spread over half the county and yet they're linked, somehow, like short stories in a book I just finished reading. I sat there watching Matt talk, watching the way his eyes looked so eager. He was saying something about not actually going down in history, that it was only an expression. He kept on talking about university and a summer job and learning how to build things, and I was hardly listening to him because I kept noticing how his face radiated some kind of energy. Joyful energy.

Tell me I didn't write that. I don't use words like joyful. There must be something wrong with this machine.

He said, "What are you going to do after high school?"

I said, "Pardon?"

"What are your plans for the future?"

"Um." I turned my head and looked out the window. The bus was slowing down, and I saw that it was my stop. He had missed his. He had actually sat there talking to me and hadn't got off at his stop. Talking to me!

He looked out, too, putting his glasses on, and said, "Oops."

He said that he'd better get off and walk back. We gathered up our stuff. There weren't many kids left on the bus, not enough to make comments, anyway. Nick, of course, got off with us and gave me a slimy leer.

Hud, as he usually did at this time of day, was hammering away on his addition. I said, "See you," to Matt, but he wasn't paying any attention to me. He started walking up the driveway toward Hud, who stopped hammering, got off his stepladder, and started looking around for something. He noticed Matt and said g'day. They exchanged a few words about the weather. "Great day."

"Cool though."

"May's to be soft. Cast your sharp eye around for my

tape measure." Matt spied it and handed it to him. "Ah. Would you hold an end, now? You're the lad."

Matt asked Hud a complicated question about joists. I headed for the house.

"Everything I know I learned helpin' Vern Dowdle. And Vern, there, he got it from Old Vern, his dad. Considered a master builder in his day, he was, Old Vern. See, here's where –"

I went in and closed the door firmly behind me.

I've got the typing job. This is what happened today, my first Saturday on my own. I went down to the Ee-lite bright and early and opened it up with the key Fran had given me. Did all the early morning chores, turned on the lights, made the coffee, made the sandwiches, blah, blah. Everything. Nobody came in. I checked supplies, started a list, organized the fridge, and still nobody came in. What was I? Typhoid Mary? They couldn't stand me. I kept looking at the clock. They hated every living hair on my head.

A woman drove into the parking lot, came in to use the washroom, and left. She could at least have bought gum. Another car pulled in, turned around, and went the other way. I looked in the mirror. Bride of Frankenstein. I was thinking of buying myself a cup of coffee so Fran wouldn't see that the day was a complete bust, but I didn't have any money.

By ten-thirty, things began to pick up. Earflaps came in. Then, around eleven, Madam Bulgy, and shortly after that Madam Bulgier. A few others I recognized came and went. A few strangers, too. It began to feel like a regular day. I got too busy to rattle and stutter. I can be pretty efficient when I get going.

It turns out Earflaps is a retired carpenter. Old Vern Dowdle, by name, the one Hud mentioned. Old Vern told me that when his wife died last fall, he started coming in for coffee and the occasional meal. Young Vern, his son, moved to Kingston two years ago, so he has no family close by. "Nothing quite as lonely as a boiled egg for supper," he said when he told me this, "unless it's half a tin of soup." He said, "I come in almost every day, for if I don't, Fran's on the phone there calling me up to make sure I ain't died in my sleep. I don't like to worry her. Oh, it's a terrible responsibility to others to be old, you know."

Madam Bulgy has a name, too. Ruby McKericher. The other lady is her sister, Pearl Hurlehey. They meet clan-destinely (I love the thesaurus key on this machine) at the Ee-lite at a set time every few days because their husbands hate each other and have vowed out-and-out family warfare if anyone in the family tries to patch things up. Pearl Hurlehey isn't on the phone and lives way up back of Ambrose deep in the bush somewhere. Boy, the things you learn! I hate to admit that I'm interested in all this junk.

I'm turning into a sponge, soaking up other people's lives. I didn't even think about other people *having* lives. Up until today, they didn't even have names. Old Vern worrying about Fran being worried about him, and the two sisters, Ruby and Pearl, risking their necks just for a chance to ask each other's advice about their married daughters and reminisce about their childhoods and tell each other where the bargains are. It's almost as if they're all connected somehow. They make me think of the inside of my computer.

About the typing job. One of the strangers who came in was a gray-haired gentlemanly type. Very polite. Spoke with rounded vowels, like somebody on CBC Radio. He sat down at one of the tables near the window, and when I went over to take his order he introduced himself as Grainger Cleary. He was in the area, doing research he said. He'd dropped in on Mrs. Bellington to make further arrangements about his summer living accommodations. "Young Matthew told me that you would do some typing for me," he said, "and that I would find you here if I wanted to discuss the job with you. You come highly recommended."

"Cark," I replied. Good Lord.

"I can't afford to pay you a great deal." He told me how much, but I was so busy trying to get my voice working, I forgot to listen to the amount.

"Would that be all right?" he asked.

I nodded. Tiny wires inside my throat were being tightened against my voice box. Soon trickles of blood would drool from the corners of my mouth. He asked for coffee and I brought it to him, gripping cup and saucer firmly with both hands.

He had a battered old brown briefcase on the floor beside him. "If you want," he said, "you could start with this." He hauled out about a hundred pages of handwriting on lined yellow paper. "Do you think you'll be able to read it?"

I looked closely at it. I wasn't even sure it was in English. Page after page of ancient Egyptian hieroglyphics. I began to recognize a word or two. And. The. Rural communities. Existence of. Ghosts? I looked up at him and then down again at his writing. Something, something, "belief in the existence of ghosts is more commonly prevalent among people of English, Scottish, and Irish ancestry who have retained their" – something, something.

"Ghosts?" I whispered, sounding haunted without intending to.

"Yes," he said. "It's part of a study I'm doing. Actually, you might find it quite interesting. It's amazing how many people have ghost stories to tell. Particularly in this area."

"You're writing a book about ghosts?" My voice worked.

"So it would appear."

"Nobody believes in ghosts." I looked at him.

He stirred sugar into his coffee and placed the spoon carefully on the edge of the saucer. "I think that rather depends on what you mean by ghosts. If you forget Hollywood and the comic-book versions of ghosts, I think you'll find that memories, fears, longings, strong passions, all that sort of thing, are related to ghostly emanations." He swallowed some coffee. He smiled at me then, as if tossing away what he'd just said. "Don't worry. I'm only asking you to type it, not believe it or understand it."

He left me with the fat pile of handwritten pages tucked into a yellow envelope. I told him I didn't yet have a printer but intended to get one as soon as I could afford it. We exchanged phone numbers and he paid for his coffee, took his bricfcase, and opened the cafe door to leave. It was one of those breezy spring afternoons when clouds are shifted across the sky as if the world is being rearranged. Sun beating down on the asphalt parking lot made it smell like both the future and the past. I will regret that statement, probably. If I reread it later I'll have serious doubts about my sanity. Right now I know what it means. The smell of hot asphalt reminds me of summer, past summers. I know the smell. But I've never smelled this one in summer. It's still in the future, and yet I think I've already been there. The ghost thing is going to be weird. I'm turning this machine off.

Wait. One more thing. Grainger Cleary stood in the doorway for a few seconds. Ruby McKericher and her sister, Pearl Hurlehey, had run out of things to say to each other the moment Cleary entered the place. Old Vern Dowdle had gone home too soon, missing the entire afternoon's performance. Anyway, he stood in the doorway as if he were thinking about something. "If you want to hold off on the printer," he said, "I think I can bring quite a nice one you can borrow when I come back on Victoria Day weekend." I agreed and saw my little vision of myself striding across the vast white tundra getting closer.

"Nothing new about ghosts," Ruby said to Pearl after he'd gone. "'Member Grandma Cooch?"

"Only what I've been told."

Ruby looked at me. "The skirt of her was all you could see, but Grandma Cooch it was without question, comin' down the ladder out of the loft, one step and then another step and another. Oh, my. I can feel the hair on the back of my arms, just thinking."

It's very late. I'm glad I can hear Hud snoring. I might leave the lamp beside my bed turned on.

6

he twenty-fourth of May, the Queen's birthday. If we don't get a holiday, we'll all run away." Ma felt she had to brighten our day with this little rhyme at breakfast this morning. First time in my life I'd ever heard it, but not, as it soon became apparent, the last. Josh said, "Say it again." So she did. Then Hud, outside examining his seed potatoes, rattled it off as if he'd invented it, and even a guy on the radio going on about Queen Victoria turned it into something like rap. Where, I want to know, does the past leave off and the future start? Queen Victoria! I want to get into the future, but I keep getting distracted by the past and bogged down in the present. Bogged down is absolutely right. Planting. Some holiday. Up at the crack. Out on the land to moil and toil. Bloody slave labor they have going for them. I've never planted anything in my life before this morning. You take these little brown specks and shriveled crumbs and old used beans, all dead, shove them into the mud, and apparently wait. Then voilà. Dinner. Eventually.

"Quicker to go into town to the supermarket," I said.

"Where do you think the stuff in the supermarket comes from?" Hud said.

Does he think I'm stupid? I mean, I know this. Although I've never spent much time thinking about the beginnings of things, I guess.

"Everything has to start somewhere," he said.

Ghost-writing, I mean typing Mr. Cleary's ghost manuscript, is beginning to affect me. Why am I starting to care about the past, and why is the future getting so fuzzy? I think I'm losing touch with reality.

This is reality. Ruth came here yesterday, Sunday, for part of the long weekend. Not here, precisely. She stayed at Bellcroft Manor, Matt's mother's bed 'n' brekkie. She wanted to come, she said, because she needs a change of scenery and because she wants to see how things are going for me, and it's totally unrelated to her job. She's just interested in my welfare. Good Lord.

I went over there on the Huddlestons' bike Sunday afternoon to see if she'd arrived. I could have phoned, but I didn't want to run the risk of going voiceless if Matt answered. Or I could have waited until she called me.

So why didn't I? I never used to be this curious.

After forcing down more of Ma's meatloaf sandwiches than I ever thought I could, I sneaked away while Josh was in the bathroom. I hate the way he always wants to be involved in every aspect of my so-called life. Edith-Ann took an interest in me when I got the bike out of the barn, as if she might follow me, but changed her mind. I wouldn't have minded if she had. Silent company.

I pedaled the Huddlestons' bicycle along the narrow road, glancing around, noticing how delicate, almost shy, the trees looked, scantily clad in their new leaves. The sun felt toasty, comforting. On one side of the road were fields so newly green they made some part of me, not my eyes, ache.

This machine's gone wacko!

Start again. It was hot enough to make my shirt stick to my back. Black flies or gnats or something kept getting into my ears and hair. I have forty thousand bites. Those little suckers take chunks out of you. One of the fields was dotted with sheep, no doubt the Huddlestons'. I haven't bothered to explore the extent of the farm, but it seems to include more than what you can see from the house. I know that when Hud goes fence-checking he looks pretty tired when he gets back.

Riding along, I could hear the monotonous bleating of sheep in the field. On the other side of the road, beyond a decrepit split-rail fence, the view of what might be a lake was hidden by clumps of scrub cedar and a run of pinkish gray rock that rose in meandering steps, then disappeared behind a spread of juniper. I crossed an intersection, passed the Ee-lite, and turned right into a dirt road. Almost immediately, I reached a hedge of lilacs drooping with deep purple flower clusters, some past their bloom. Through a space in the hedge lay a private road with a wooden sign at its entrance announcing Bellcroft Manor. La-de-da. I aimed the bike through the dark opening and coasted down the winding lane.

What a bizarre place Bellcroft Manor is! I jammed on the brakes when I caught sight of the house – I mean, mansion. It was built in a valley, sunk, really, in a craterlike dip of land and almost overpowered by spiked sentinels of evergreens. Beyond it, the land rolled uphill to over-look the lake. I got off the bike and walked it, ducking under the low swaying branches of a weeping willow shading the drive that curved around the front of the house. I propped the bike against the thick trunk and studied the place through the leaves that drooped like tat-tered lace. The clapboard house rose like the three tiers of an abandoned wedding cake. Slatted wooden chairs sprawled on a sagging front veranda. To the right in the distance the lake shimmered, and at the back the cracked and crumbling edge of a tennis court caught my eye. It looked like some old resort going to seed. The last resort. I crossed the veranda and pressed the doorbell. There was no sound. I pressed it again and got the same result.

I went around the corner of the house looking for evi-dence of habitation. Upstairs the window blinds were pulled, but on the top tier, a window was open and a curtain rippled in the breeze. Shielding my eyes against the sun, I glimpsed a groundhog in the middle of the lawn sitting tall on his haunches, apparently the only resident. He scuttled down his hole when I moved on around to the back of the house. I found another door.

My excuse is that I was looking for Ruth. But what I did next, there's no excuse for. I creaked up the back-porch steps to the door. Before knocking I looked through the window in the door, framed by white curtains, like the doors Josh draws when he draws a house.

There was Matt, beside him a kitchen table loaded with silver things – bowls, a teapot, platterlike dishes, I don't know what all, candleholder things. He definitely did not look happy. His mother (I figured it was his mother, graying hair pulled into a roll at the back, attractive sort of, tired-looking) came into view. They were obviously arguing about the stuff on the table. She handed him a jar of something, polish maybe. He put it down. She handed him a cloth. He tossed it onto the table. I was loving this.

I couldn't hear everything they said, but I could make out some of it. I caught their tones. She wanted the silver polished, and he thought it was a waste of time. "Appearances are important," I heard her say. "We can't just let things go."

"We've let the veranda go until it's about to fall off the front of the house. I should be putting blocks under it."

She turned partly away from him and swept the back of her hand across her forehead.

He said, quite reasonably I thought, "I should be taking out some of those trees. Let some light in here."

His mother remained motionless for a moment and then began to droop, looking dejected. He glanced over at her and down at the silver. He muttered something and started taking the lid off the polish. She brightened. He didn't.

I was just stepping away from the window when I saw her attack him with an apron, which she forced over his head and around his waist. Ruffled. Mauve. He tried to push it away, although not very strenuously. She tied it at his back – the winner. His face lost its expression – the loser. Dully, he looked straight ahead. Right into my prying face.

I could have died. I should have died. I ran down the porch steps and back around to the front of the house. I grabbed the bicycle away from the tree trunk and strained every muscle I had getting up the lane again and out to the road just as Ruth's car turned in.

I waved and kept going.

She stuck her head through her open window and called something to me.

"Phone me," I yelled and pedaled like mad.

What had I done? Me! The world's most private person! Invading someone else's private life! If I were Matt, I would never look me in the face again. Certainly never sit beside me on the bus. In fact, I would develop such a deep aversion to someone like me that I would backspace me right out of existence.

I pedaled hard to put some distance between me and Matt. It didn't take a psychology course to see that Lady B., as they call her down at the Ee-lite, was doing some kind of smothering-mothering guilt thing on him. And he wasn't standing up to it very well. That ruffled apron.

Mauve. If I hated him, it would be a good thing to drag up for taunting purposes. If I hated him.

He probably hates me, now. Of course he does. This is the sort of thing I know all about. Let somebody peek through a crack in your box, see you when you've sunk to your lowest, and boy, they've had it. When I step out of my glass box I show one face to the world, and one face only. Nobody sees Sara Moone at her worst.

Why would I care if he hates me? I've never shown any indication of liking him. The way he talks. He sounds so . . . I mean, good-looking guys like that are always so . . . I mean, I can't stand the guy.

On the day of my sixteenth birthday, I will get on a bus and head north to a city. Any city. I'll get a full-time job, maybe in a store. I can live over the store. I can see myself living alone in a cozy room over a store. Every day I will go to work down below, and every evening I'll climb back up to my room and write, not day-to-day things, but mysteries. Without ghosts. I hate ghosts. Murder mysteries. I will not allow any person to mess up my world. Then, when I've saved enough money, I'm heading up the map to the true north, strong and free. To fly in the sky and in my spare time write books. I'll be a hermit in the northern wilds with no means of communication. The mysterious hermit mystery writer. Famous for it. Known far and wide. "Tess of the Tundra." Maybe I'll think of a better title.

Those are the things I was thinking on the way back home. On the way back to the Huddlestons' farm, I mean. Matt was a thing of the past. Deleted.

I was biking along, starting to feel better, trying not to think about Ruth and what I would answer if she asked me why I'd taken off like a bat out of hell. At the top of a steep hill I came to the field of sheep again and stopped to catch my breath. I straddled my bike, watching them. From this distance they looked like cuddly toys, noses to the ground, munching their way through the green field. Through the cedars on the other side of the road I could smell the freshness of the lake in the distance. The combination of warm sun touching my head and fresh breezes lifting my hair made it hard to focus on snow drifting across ice.

"Sheep may safely graze," I said out loud. Babbling. The result of sunstroke, probably. It was from some hymn or an anthem or something I remembered from one of the many churches I had been subjected to. Religion has never made a large impact on my muddled life. In one church I was just nicely placed safe in the arms of Jesus when I was uprooted and carted off to another church, where I was assured of an eternity of hellfire and damnation. It was the organ music and the choir singing in the "Sheep May Safely Graze" church that I remember most vividly. Right now, I had an odd sense of something comforting in the reality of woolly sheep and the endless green field all safely encompassed by the rail fence. This comfort thing was distressing. I tried for the tundra again, but it failed me.

I put my foot on the raised pedal, about to start off, but noticed that a rail near the corner of the field closest to the road was broken. The two snapped ends lay together on the ground, leaving a V-shaped hole probably big enough for a curious sheep to stumble through. I set off.

I went directly into the house. I could see through the kitchen window that Hud and Nick were planting potatoes. Hud was planting. Nick, his shirt tied around his skinny waist, was leaning on a spade. Josh was there, too, stepping on hills they'd just formed, falling over marker stakes at the edges of the garden. I should have been out there helping, probably, but I had things to say to this machine. Ma came in just as I was heading for the stairs. She had to get the bread she was baking out of the oven. The aroma in the kitchen was enough to make anyone dizzy. Quickly, before she could start in about bread-baking and planting and life in general, I said, "Could you tell Hud there's a hole in the fence where the sheep are? I have to go upstairs."

"Oh Lord love a duck," Ma said, washing her hands at the sink. She grabbed potholders and opened the oven door. "What next I wonder sure if it's not one thing it's about five hundred others not a day goes by but what –"

I escaped.

Safe in my room with my door shut, I just nicely got this machine going when I heard Ma hollering at me. Is there no peace anywhere? My machine refuses to give answers. All it can do is save and exit.

I opened my bedroom door to find out what Ma wanted.

"You got a friend here to see you," she said from the bottom of the stairs. I waited for more but, surprisingly, she stopped. What did she mean, a friend? I don't have any. Ruth appeared behind Ma, looking more like a real person than a social worker. I wouldn't go so far as to describe her as a friend.

"Hi," she said.

"You go right on up," Ma said to Ruth. "Sara keeps her room all nice and tidy so's you could invite the queen of England in if you had a mind and sure you'd never be a bit ashamed if you did and there's cookies down here in the jar Sara you know where they are and don't let Miss Petrie go with her tongue hangin' out for lack of a bite of something sweet and I'll be out in the garden if you need me." Ruth climbed the stairs with the skirt of her green dress flaring out around her like long grass.

"Nice," she said, looking around my closet-sized room. A breeze through the window rustled the pale curtains. I glanced around and noticed the way the sun, peeping through a newly leafed maple at the side of the house, dappled the wallpaper, highlighting the pattern. Violets and daisies. I had never actually noticed the pattern until this moment.

"Bit small," I said.

"Cozy."

"Cozy? I suppose it is." Now that I thought about it.

"What's this?" Ruth asked. She lifted the framed embroidery out from the wall where it hung facing in and squinted underneath at the words. She looked at me out of the corner of her eye and, nodding, put it back. "Just about says it all, doesn't it?" she said.

I cast her a narrow-eyed glare. I gave Ruth the chair and sat on the bed, inching back to lean against the wall. Now what, I wondered. What do you do with a social worker who thinks she's a friend sitting in your room? "Could use some rain," I said. Good Lord. I was beginning to sound like Hud or somebody.

Leaning an elbow on my desk with her knuckles on the side of her head, she was frowning at the back of the embroidery. She muttered, "That bothers me!"

I glanced at it noncommittally.

"She put it there for you, you know." When I didn't respond, she shook her head and changed the subject. "I was wondering why you ran away just as I arrived at Bellcroft."

"No reason. I didn't run away. I just sort of left."

"The Bellingtons are nice."

"If you like that sort of thing."

"Good-looking boy."

I gave her my bored-to-the-point-of-self-destruction look. She asked me about my typing job, so I showed her the stack of handwriting I had recently finished deciphering. It's stored in my computer until Grainger lends me a printer.

"This looks pretty interesting," she said after reading a page of it. She glanced at another page. "Listen to this. 'Where traditional cultures remain intact and largely untouched by modern society, phenomena hold a certain status. Their occurrence and recurrence are considered manifestations of strong personalities. It is believed that in life, they evoked such strong passions of love, fear, hatred, or longing within families and communities that they return bidden or unbidden like memories.'" She looked at the title page. "Grainger Cleary! That's the man I nearly flattened with my car!"

"You're a menace to society, Ruth."

"I didn't see him when I was parking my car at Bellcroft. And suddenly he reared up in front of the windshield. Scared me half out of my wits."

"In your hands, a steering wheel becomes a lethal weapon."

"I didn't touch him."

"There's always tomorrow."

"He's very polite. Introduced himself."

"Know your adversary, I always say."

"He seemed awfully nice."

"Doomed."

She seemed to think our conversation wasn't going anywhere and suggested we go outside. Before leaving, she turned the framed thing to face out. I gave her my sugariest smile.

And turned it back in.

Ma met us at the bottom of the stairs with lemonade and some glasses. "I was just about to call up and here you are like you could read my mind for I thought we could all do with a cool drink on a day like this especially Hud for he'll never quit unless I tie him down and sit on him not that I –" I opened the door for Ma and we went out.

Hud remarked that this wasn't getting the work done,

but he didn't seem to care that much because he sat in the shade of the maple and downed two glasses. Nick complained because it wasn't Coke, and Josh tripped over Nick's foot, spilling half his lemonade on Nick's arm, so Nick swore and pushed him and Josh wailed and Hud roared at the two of them. A normal day.

Ma went back in to slice some bread.

"How are things going?" Ruth asked Hud.

"Not bad," he said. He looked over at me with that sort of relaxed smile he has. "Got a little plantin' done. See what comes up."

Hard to tell whether he was talking about me or the garden, nodding his head and contemplating me the way he had examined his seed potatoes earlier.

Ma brought out a plate of sliced and buttered bread still warm from the oven, and a dish of maple syrup to dip it in. For which there is no earthly equivalent, I freely admit it.

I asked Hud if he'd heard about the broken fence.

"Yep," he said. "Just about to go down and do something about it." He got up stiffly. "Cre-ea-k," he groaned, straightening his back.

"Wait up," Josh called after him. "I'm coming, too. I need to bring back a lamb. Wanna keep one in my room."

Ma said, among other things, that it would be over her dead body. She collected the glasses and took them inside to wash them. Ruth asked if she needed some help, but Ma said no, among other things.

"I really like your family," Ruth said to me.

"My family?" I looked at Ma balancing a tray of glasses expertly in one hand, posing like a little square ballerina while she opened the kitchen door. I watched Hud's departing back and Josh running, stopping, bending to pick something up to show Hud and Hud shaking his head. Josh throwing away whatever it was and then clambering up Hud's sturdy side to be given a piggyback ride. Hud stooping to hoist him up and then straightening with some difficulty. "Ton o' bricks," we heard him say. Two kittens scampered along behind. Edith-Ann felt moved to get up and follow at a discreet distance. I looked at Nick sitting apart, crouched, leaning against the cool bricks of the house, shifting his eyes away when I looked at him. I'd never really thought in terms of family before.

And I'm not about to start now.

That all happened yesterday. I think I'm addicted to this machine. Now I have to finish writing up today. I will be brief. It's the twenty-fourth of May, or the next best thing to it, the queen's birthday, and we all got a Monday holiday after the garden was planted, even Hud, so nobody ran away. Yet. Soon, though.

Ma splurged and bought firecrackers. "Waste of money," Hud said, but he watched them with the rest of us, quite a crowd, as a matter of fact.

Ruth came over again Monday afternoon before leaving for home. Ma insisted on inviting her to stay for supper and watch the fireworks. "It's only shepherd's pie," Ma said, "but there's plenty of it plus there's bread and I'll put together a salad and we have enough apple crumb to feed a small army for a week so if you'd like to –"

"I'd love to, thanks. My mother used to make shepherd's pie."

"What kind of pie?" I asked.

"Did she now and what would she put in it I always add carrots myself and of course mounds of potatoes and never scrimp on the meat but you'd know that at least your mother would and drain the meat well –"

"What kind of pie is this?"

"My mother often used leftover meat."

"Oh that makes up real nice no question but to my mind the best meat is –"

"If shepherd's pie is about eating sheep, I'm going to vomit."

"No dear," Ma said, "hamburger's your man every time nice and lean but with a little fat for flavor and a clove or two of chopped garlic my neighbor Mrs. Oaksi puts in five but I think –"

On and on they went, through every variation of every recipe made by every cook they'd ever known. We don't discuss why the sheep are raised. They have wool. That much we know. The closest we came was when Josh asked Hud what going to market meant. He sat Josh down, took one of his bare feet in his big calloused hands and started, "This little piggie went to market; this little piggie stayed home; this little piggie had roast beef; this little piggie had none, and this little piggie cried wee-wee-wee all the way home." I repeat the whole thing because I'd never heard it before and it kind of looked like – well, fun. For a little kid, that is.

"Do it again," Josh kept demanding, "do it again." By the time Hud had finished doing the whole rhyme four times on each foot we still didn't know what going to market meant. But we didn't give a damn, either.

How did I get off on that? Throughout the entire supper Nick kept sucking up to Ruth, trying to charm the living life right out of her. She seemed puzzled, but I wasn't. He's got something up his sleeve. God knows what. When she said she'd better go back to Bellcroft for her suitcase and leave from here after the fireworks, he asked if he could go along for the ride. She turned him down – politely – but turned him down, nevertheless. Not sure why I was glad. It's not as if Ruth is important to me.

Ruth returned just as it was becoming dusk, but not alone. Behind hers was another car. Grainger Cleary got out one side and Matthew Bellington the other.

Then all kinds of politeness. Ruth saying to Hud and Ma, I hope you don't mind; Grainger saying how very kind, very pleased to meet you, very this, very that, blah blah. Matt not opening his yap.

Grainger took this big printer out of the back of his car, and a couple of stacks of paper. I carried it all up to my room and would have stayed to attach the printer to my machine to test it out, but Ma was calling me to come back down.

Ma handed around mosquito lotion. "They come out

in full force at a quarter to nine sure you could set your clock by them and take a lawn chair not that there's such an awful lot of firecrackers for they're a dreadful price but still I've got the egg money I like to keep for treats and would you not have brought your mother?" This last was directed at Matt.

He said, "Oh. She's pretty busy."

We sat at the side of the house just beyond the new part. Hud hasn't had time to do much work on it lately, so it's reached a bit of a standstill. Ma opened a lawn chair and so did Ruth. Grainger started to put his next to Ruth's, but Nick wedged himself on the ground between them. This didn't stop Grainger from talking to Ruth. Talking is hardly the word. Interviewing would be more like it. He seemed to be interested in her entire life history. She'll turn up as a ghost in his book if she's not careful. I've never seen Ruth quite so lively. She's fairly serene, usually, when she's not behind the wheel of a car. But in conversation with Grainger, she was something else entirely. She sparkled and bubbled as if someone had popped her cork.

I sat way back on the framework of the addition. I'm not afraid of fireworks, exactly. I know it's just a few sparks, a bang, a poof, and it's over. It has nothing to do with blazing or burning. Except for the smell. The smell almost makes me gag. Matt leaned against one of the studs near where I was perched.

Getting the show started, Hud set a bucket of sand on the edge of the hill just before it slopes down out of sight.

All you could see behind him were the tops of some apple trees growing down the slope and the cloud-streaked sky stained in layers of pink and purple and finally inky blue. Josh ran back and forth like a dog with a ball from Ma to Hud until Hud bent to light the first firecracker anchored in the sand and Ma nabbed Josh, holding him tight to watch.

The fuse caught and sputtered. I held my breath. Hud stood back out of the way. Comets whistled up out of the bucket, cascading into a shower of sparks, and Ruth clapped. So did Josh. Ma cheered. I let my breath out.

And there was Hud standing on the edge of the universe like God creating the stars and the moon.

"Why were you looking through our kitchen door yesterday?" Matt asked me. He was looking at the next shower of comets.

I was going to deny that it was me but said um, instead. "I thought I was seeing ghosts."

"Sorry," I said. "I didn't really see you."

"That's funny. You were looking right at me."

What a strange guy, standing there, hands in his pockets, not angry, not embarrassed, not looking at me. I said, "I mean, I didn't notice anything." Something called a Roman candle, Hud announced, burned without fanfare, turning the hillside eerily green.

"Notice anything?" Matt looked at me now. Josh was yelling at Hud to make one go bang. "What was there to notice?"

"Nothing."

"Come on. You must have noticed something, or you wouldn't be denying noticing anything. My mother and I arguing about polishing silver? We argue about everything. What do you mean?"

A red star popped over the brow of the hill. Then a green one. *Pop!* Josh yelled for more.

"What didn't you notice?" Matt insisted. *Pop!* A silver one. He was staring down at me as if he'd keep asking forever.

"The apron." I kept my voice low.

"Apron?" He looked as though he were searching his memory. "The apron. So what about it?"

"Sorry if I embarrassed you." I couldn't believe that was me apologizing. Normally I hate that. I was thinking about how frail Frank wouldn't have been caught dead in an apron, and old Arn, good Lord, if Sonia had tried to stick one over his head, she'd have ended up with a broken jaw.

"I guess I don't embarrass easily." Matt laughed.

I felt like someone from some bizarre foreign country with a language no one wants to speak and customs people try to ignore. I went over and sat on the ground beside Ma.

The fireworks didn't last long. "Awww," Josh complained after the last one. "Awww, one more. Come on. Awww." It didn't do him any good.

"Look at the moon, Josh," Grainger said. And we all looked up at an unimpressive new moon with a dark shape almost surrounding it. Grainger said:

I saw the new moon late yestreen
Wi' the auld moon in her arm;
And if we gang to sea, master,
I fear we'll come to harm.

"What's he talking like that for?" Josh asked Hud.

"To keep you from whining prob'ly. See the new moon up there? Looks like she's luggin' the old one around with her."

Ma was looking up, too, and said, "I hope it's just an old saying for I don't want any of us to come to harm but it's sure to mean rain which is what we need now that the garden's in."

Everybody started to leave. Grainger stood over Ruth shaking her hand and looking down at her. He's tall; Ruth isn't. She was staring up at him with some kind of look in her eyes. I have a great urge to say she looked enchanted, but I don't use words like enchanted. I don't know how she looked; it was dark. Hud and Matt were having a deep conversation. Edith-Ann came out of hiding and went up to Ruth. "Don't pat the dog," I said.

Ruth asked, "Why not?"

"She bites."

"Oh." Ruth bent and patted her anyway, and Edith-Ann wagged her tail.

Good Lord.

Ma said to Matthew as he was getting into the car, "I guess the bed-and-breakfast business is doing pretty good these days."

"Getting better and better," he said. "A woman called today to book a room for the first two weeks in July."

"Well now –"

"A repeat customer like Mr. Cleary."

"The best kind," Cleary said, getting into the driver's side.

"She came one weekend in the winter. I had to go over and pick her up at the cafe where the bus let her off," Matt said.

I remembered the occasion.

Matt continued, "She's coming by car this time. I think she said she has a daughter living nearby."

They all left waving. I have an impression of Matt with his head out the car window smiling, maybe at me, but probably not. Hard to tell in the dark. He has a very open and generous face so that when he smiles at you, you feel as if you're getting a gift. I heard the good-byes, the see you-soons, and Ma calling us in, echoing around inside my head while I stood, not moving. Over it all buzzed the words "a daughter nearby, a daughter nearby," until my head was filled to the bursting point. The two cars driving away must have taken all the light with them.

I stood in the dark and shivered.

CHAPTER

7

I scrolled up the last few paragraphs and nearly deleted them. I didn't, however, because it wouldn't make any difference. The woman will come whether or not I include her in this machine's memory. She has her own story, and it isn't part of mine. She is simply some unrelated woman who happens to have a daughter in the vicinity. Every female in this county is some woman's daughter. Let her come. I've stopped thinking about her.

I have only three more weeks of school before I write my last exam (and I do mean last). No more school, ever. Except for flying school. I'll be glad to have more time to work on Grainger's manuscript. He said I could correct any spelling and punctuation errors I found. I love that kind of thing. I hooked up the printer he lent me and printed out fifty pages for him. He seemed pleased with the work. Fran wants me to work Wednesdays as well as Saturdays and help her out during the summer when it gets busy. I think I'll have plenty of cash to head north with. Just looking at a map of Ontario, I think my best bet would be to go northwest from here to Timmins, work for a while in a store, and then go either north to Moose Factory or west and north to Pickle Lake. Not too many roads up there. Oh, well.

Josh got a birthday card from his mother in the mail today. Ma showed it to him at suppertime. He started tearing around all excited, asking when he was going to get his presents and his cake with candles and could he have firecrackers, too, because what about that queen lady who got them on her birthday, so why couldn't he?

"It's not really your birthday yet, sweetie," Ma said. "Not till the middle of September, which is when the leaves start to change colors so's you'll know when it's coming."

He slowed down and finally ground to a halt. He stared at the card. "Well, how come I got this birthday card then?" This little squatty kid looking up at Ma for the truth and Ma chewing on her bottom lip wondering what to tell him. "How come?" He studied the card as if the dog in a cowboy hat sitting on a horse could provide the answer to this mystery.

"You'd think she'd know when his birthday is," Nick said.

"'Spect she got muddled up," Hud said.

"'Spect she got stoned," Nick muttered, but Hud didn't hear him.

Josh looked inside the card and at the back but couldn't find any clues. Hud was giving him his soft look, and Ma was telling him he could have two pieces of pie for dessert. "I guess I only like cat cards anyways," Josh said. He took the card and put it under a pile of newspapers beside the washing machine.

"She's coming to get you," Nick whispered in his ear and ran before Josh could work up a good gob of spit.

Now that the hens have gone into full production, Ma makes us collect eggs. Josh is pretty good at it. He has names for the hens – Softy, Rosabell, Four-wheel-drive (don't ask me why), Spot, and Mookie are some of them. He walks bravely up to them sitting on their nests, calls them by name, asks how they're feeling, reaches under them, and grabs the eggs. I couldn't do that. I take a broomhandle and nudge them off the nest. Those accusing eyes! Those wicked beaks! If they flap their wings at me, I nearly have a stroke.

Nick is even more frightened of them than I am, I think, although he pretends he isn't. He yells at them and rushes at them. One flew at him and I think he would have kicked it if I hadn't been watching.

Hud has hired Matt Bellington to help him. I haven't seen him on the bus lately because his exams are finished. I got home from school yesterday to a scene of renewed activity on the addition. Josh was there hammering bent nails into scraps of wood. One of his cats sat nearby, washing her ears in the sun, waiting for his undivided attention. Nick sidled into the house so that nobody could nab him to help just seconds before Hud came puffing around the corner of the house toting one end of a pile of boards. The other end was being hoisted by Matt, who nearly dropped it when he said hello.

"Thought we could use some hired help around here for a month or two," Hud said as if I had requested an explanation. "Take yer end there and lay her right down in the corner," he said to Matt.

Inside Ma started in. "What he's going to pay that lad with is beyond me for it's not like we have money growin' on trees but you know Hud softhearted as they come and soft in the head too I sometimes think when it comes to kids needing things even if it's only a summer job but who am I to find fault when I know Hud likes to do a good turn when he can and he used to work up there at Bellingtons when old Bellington the grandfather was alive as I did myself at one time and my mother before me course he should have a strong lad to help for he's been lookin' peaked the last few days I think don't you?"

Hard to tell with Hud. He's like the earth under you. It's always there holding you up, so you don't pay much attention to how it looks. "Maybe he needs a vacation," I said.

"He tried that once about ten years ago but it didn't take. We went out to his sister's place way out in Moose Jaw Saskatchewan out west. They have a farm. First morning Jimmy, his brother-in-law, puts his boots on and goes out and Hud he sits there with a newspaper and he turns over every page in it and says there isn't the same kind of news as we have back home and he keeps lookin' out the window kind of and pacing around until Betty says, that's his sister, take Jimmy's other pair of boots for I think they'll fit and off he goes and works just as hard as ever he did at home and that was the last vacation he ever took."

Classes are over, so I'm home studying for exams. Next year's courses look pretty interesting. Physics. Ancient history. I won't be around to take them, of course, so I don't know why I'm even thinking about them.

Hard to escape Matt, now that he works for Hud. I'd like to. I'm not in his world. He doesn't know that an apron could be worth a broken jaw or getting an argument from a bossy woman means you throw stuff at her. Hard to know how to act with that type of person. Where's his boiling point? Best to leave a big blank space between him and me.

This morning I was finishing my breakfast when it started to rain. Hud and Matt came in to wait out the shower, drinking coffee while I loaded breakfast dishes into the dishwasher. Josh attached himself to Matt and demanded to be read to from his favorite book, the fall and winter Canadian Tire catalog. Matt pushed his glasses up higher on his nose and obliged. He didn't seem to find it a peculiar choice of reading material. He read him snowblowers and sounded almost as excited about them as Josh was. He was going to start table saws when the rain let up and Hud said, "All hands on deck. That means you, too, mister," he said to Nick, who sat shuffling and reshuffling a deck of cards, making no move to join the work party. "If you're not studying for exams, you're outside pulling your share. Which is it to be?"

"I studied already. I know it all."

"Get on out there, then."

Nick said, "But I'm still hungry. I haven't finished breakfast." He looked at Ma.

Ma said, "He'll be along sure he can't do much on an empty stomach and it's his turn to collect the eggs. He'll be along." She put two pieces of bread in the toaster and began to peel an orange for him.

Good Lord.

I should have gone into town to study in the library. This place was like a crisis center after a national disaster. Briefly: Nick came howling in from the henhouse, having been attacked by a ferocious gang of chickens. He demanded to be taken to the doctor; Ma said they hadn't even broken the skin. He screamed at her, grabbed a paring knife from the kitchen counter, and stabbed it into his arm. "Now are you satisfied?" he yelled at Ma, blood pouring out and dripping off the point of his elbow.

We were all in the kitchen by now. Nick screaming, Ma babbling trying to comfort him, Hud roaring for everyone to calm down, Josh so scared he wet his pants all over the floor, and Matt. Matt said to me, "Have you got any Band-Aids?"

I found some, but Nick wouldn't let anyone near him. Hud got him calmed down eventually, and they went into town to the hospital emergency department. I cleaned up the floor, Ma cleaned up Josh, and Matt went back outside to hammer nails.

Try and get the entire French Revolution into your head following that. I closed my books.

Ma came into my room, something she seldom does, probably because I tend to glare at people who take liberties with my privacy. She sat on the edge of my bed, her short arms folded across her front, hardly able to reach. She sat like that, looking at the wall. I don't know whether she noticed the embroidery turned backward.

"What?" I said. I was still sitting at my desk.

She didn't say anything, just shook her head. Ma with nothing to say was a Ma to be concerned about. I waited.

"We're not doing him any good."

"Nick?"

"He's getting worse, not better."

"Maybe he wants to go live with his mother."

Ma looked at me now. "He hasn't got a mother. She was a drug addict and oh she looked after him off and on when she could but mostly she pawned him off on some friend or a sister no better than herself or anyone would feed him and finally she died of a drug overdose with him beside her and that's how they found him a little kid clinging to his dead mother which I can't bear to think about and the Lord only knows how long she was dead because he was half starved so he was and only six years old and nothing we do here seems to make that go away." Big tears rolled down Ma's cheeks and when she talked her words came out in gulps. I pictured myself going over to her, sitting on the edge of the bed beside her, putting an arm around her.

I didn't, of course.

She left, finally.

After a while I went downstairs. Through the kitchen window I saw Ma outside sitting in a lawn chair. It wasn't any kind of a day for sitting out – gray, fog to the point almost of drizzle. There was Ma, staring off into space, and there was Edith-Ann with her head in Ma's lap and Ma's arm across her back.

I went back up to my room and turned her needlework around.

When I start erasing all I've put into this computer, this is where I'll begin.

Exams are over. School's finished. I'm getting closer to freedom every day. I had a look at next year's physics textbook, just to see if there was anything in it I couldn't live without. There was stuff on computers, a couple of chapters on aerodynamics. A few other things. I don't care, though.

I wrote to the Chamber of Commerce in Timmins asking for information about jobs and apartments, and that kind of thing. I spend my days barricaded in my room reading, avoiding Josh, avoiding Nick, avoiding Matt (sort of), typing, helping either Hud or Ma, and working at the Ee-lite.

Another holiday today. July first, Canada's birthday. A holiday, that is, for everyone except me. And Hud, I guess. Anyway, lots of stuff going on in Ambrose – a parade, a boat show, antique cars, two rock bands, a dance, and a public fireworks display, none of which I'm going to. Fran asked me to work until four because she's busy in town helping the Lionettes sell hot dogs. So I did, and after that I went over to Bellcroft to take Grainger thirty more typed pages and to get some more handwritten ones to work on.

What a place. I know, now, why Grainger Cleary chose it. It must be haunted. When I got there, I went to the front door this time. Someone had installed a knocker, which I used, loudly. Mrs. Bellington answered. I told her who I was and why I was there, in my usual half-strangled voice. She seemed very nice, however, and invited me in. There was a dramatic change in temperature inside. The air was not just chilly, but cavelike, trapped. She went upstairs to call Grainger, who occupies the third floor.

I stood in the entry hall, gawking around, trying to breathe. The interior walls seemed to suck away my breath and exude their own damp mustiness. I'm beginning to sound like Grainger Cleary when he illustrates his observations with "true" ghost stories. Back to reality. The house was damp. I could see into the dining room, crowded and heavy with dark sideboards. Above a massive table and ornate chairs drooped a chandelier with strings of crystal droplets and dangling spears. On one side of the vast hall was a shadowy room crowded with old-fashioned furniture, its windows swathed in velvet drapery. All it needed was a braided rope cordoning it off like something in a museum. On the other side was a comfortable sitting room. This wasn't like any house I'd ever been in and definitely not like the Huddlestons'. Vacuum-packed would describe theirs, trimmed with vinyl, chrome, and imitation knotty pine.

Mrs. Bellington returned and invited me into the comfortable sitting room to wait for Grainger. Briefly I wondered where Matt might be, but soon found out from Mrs. B. that he'd gone in to town to watch the festivities. I knew Hud had given him the day off. While I was waiting, I glanced at the photographs on a table, most of them of Matt – baby Matt with no hair, toddler Matt with long curls, teenage Matt in a blazer with a crest. On the mantel were other pictures, some very old. There were photographs of a wedding, of a man in uniform, of a woman on a horse. There were old people, young people, babies and children, and all of them bore a striking resemblance to – you guessed it – Matt.

"Well, Sara. Nice to see you." Grainger making an entrance. We talked business for a while, and then he suggested we go out and sit on the veranda before we froze to death inside. Fine with me.

"Now tell me about yourself," he said when we had eased back into the slatted wooden chairs. "Satisfy my curiosity."

I shrugged. "Nothing to tell."

"For one so young you've certainly developed a very thick wall. Who are you and where do you come from? I'm incurably nosy."

"Sara. And I don't come from anywhere. I'm incurably private."

"Sara what? Be generous."

"Moone. It has an *E* on the end," I added generously. "I moved here in the winter."

"Oh. From where?"

"North Malverington."

Grainger made a face. "Not exactly paradise, is it?"

"Not exactly, but neither is Ambrose." This was a lie. Ambrose is the prettiest town I've ever seen, with its main street winding downhill to a river rushing along next to gingerbread houses and behind a castle that turns out to be the post office. I made my eyes empty circles, hoping he'd stop the third degree.

"Nice farm your folks have."

He was drawing me out. I've experienced this before from cultured people. Draw you out, then drop you flat. One foster family I had were pseudocultured types. They moved to Toronto but didn't take me.

"The people I live with are foster parents." I waited for him to look uncomfortable. I was probably the lowest form of life he'd ever spoken to.

"I thought you were adopted."

"I'm a ward of the Children's Aid." That would shut him up. I hoisted myself forward in the chair for a quick getaway.

"That's fascinating. No one ever adopted you? Sorry for being nosy, but as I said –"

"I was adopted when I was a baby, by Mr. and Mrs. Moone." I had my hands on the chair's armrests, elbows high, ready for takeoff. I could almost hear his brain clicking away like my computer keyboard, memorizing my life.

"Go on," he said.

Why would I go on? Why would I want to tell a total stranger all this junk? There are only two possible explanations. One, he had me hypnotized. Or two, I was flattered that a writer wanted to hear me talk about myself. Let's hope it was number one. Anyway, I recited what I remember of my past as if I were one of those simulated voices giving a recorded message. "Their first names are written down somewhere, but as they no longer exist, I no longer think about them. They died in an accident when I was three. A fire. I don't remember what happened; I only remember the screaming. I was almost adopted a second time by a couple who turned out to be alcoholics and therefore unacceptable as parents. I was reclaimed, then, by the Children's Aid. The alcoholics, I can remember. They swamped me with toys, some of which I still have. Then there was a bunch of places, too many – I just remember vague things – shock, fear, slaps, pinches, bad smells, boredom. Not the sort of past a person wants to dwell on."

"That's terrible!" Grainger, to give him credit, looked horrified. Probably sorry he'd asked. "How sad to be absolutely alone in the world without any family at all," he said.

I made my face a blank. The woman who had adver-tised in the newspaper looking for her daughter flashed off and on inside my head, but I erased her. "It's not so terrible," I said. "It means you've only got one person to concentrate on. It makes life easy."

"Easy! How can it be easy all by yourself?"

"I'm sorry I told you this."

"No you're not."

"What?"

"I know a haunted person when I see one."

I tried to make my eyes look empty, but I think instead they were burning into his, waiting for an explanation. I stood up, ready to escape.

He said, "You have to raise your ghosts before you can properly bury them. Some people see ghosts but won't admit it. Some people, for one reason or another, cling to their ghosts and won't relinquish them." He flipped his hand over and back. "Some, somehow, do both." He seemed to be studying me. I'll probably appear in his next book.

"Got to get back now," I said. I picked up the packet of handwritten pages he had given me and headed for my bike leaning against the tree. I stopped and turned around. I called back, "My life's not for publication. Got it?"

He waved. I hope he heard me.

That was Friday.

This is going to be painful, but I'm feeding every detail into this insatiable machine anyway. I've had a very long, very horrible day.

Bizarre things are happening. A mistake was made. I thought at first this machine was haunted, that the ghost thing was getting out of hand. But I know that the machine does not make mistakes. All errors are due to human foul-ups. Mine.

This morning, Sunday, two days after the last install-ment, Grainger phoned to say there were pages missing from his manuscript, but that there were other pages from something else, something I had obviously written. He said it looked like a diary.

I said, "Oh hell!"

"Don't worry," he said, "nothing incriminating."

I think I remember what might have happened. There were a lot of interruptions last week. I kept switching between his document and mine. Josh kept coming in bothering me and causing confusion.

Then all hell broke loose when Nick threw another fit and murdered (allegedly murdered) a chicken. Ma became hysterical. I had already printed a stack of pages but had more to do. I started the printer again and left it printing while I went to find Hud to deal with Ma and Nick. Then I grabbed the printed stuff without arranging it, without even looking at it, and put the pile of pages into Grainger's yellow envelope. A possible explanation. Or else it was ghosts.

Nick doesn't collect eggs anymore.

Anyway, Grainger said, "See if you have the missing pages one sixty-nine to one eighty, and we'll make a trade. Matt will drive over and pick you up."

"But –"

"He's on his way."

I located Grainger's missing pages, and a little while later, Matt pulled into the drive in Grainger's car.

"He could have just brought my pages here," I said.

"No, he couldn't," Matt said. "He pulled a muscle in the back of his knee and can hardly hobble around."

I got in. "How'd he do that? Ghost-busting?"

"Tennis on our battered tennis court."

We talked about that and ghosts and writing all the way to Bellcroft. I think my voice is getting better. I feel as if I'm finally in control of some part of me.

When we got there, Matt said, "I'll take you up to Grainger's Ivory Tower." We began to climb the expansive staircase, where several vintage Bellingtons gazed disapprovingly from their frames in the paneled stairwell. Generations of Bellingtons stretching back and back into history, their family name remembered.

I saw myself going up the stairs, Sara Moone, with the E tacked on for ballast, one of a kind, first person singular, taking up not quite sixteen years of time and space. Less, actually, when you think about it, considering my blank early childhood. I cannot attach myself to a history. I stand alone in the present tense.

Mrs. Bellington appeared at the bottom of the stairs,

surprised, I think, to see me with Matt. She said hello to me with just a hint of ice in her voice and made a few polite comments. Well-brought-up people must have a polite key that they press when needed and out comes the right set of phrases. Then she asked Matt if he could try to open the stuck window in the large guest room.

"I may need your help at some point this afternoon," she said pointedly to Matt. "We have a guest arriving today, remember."

At a landing partway up, the stairs branched, one way leading up to the main section of the house, another through a door to a short flight of stairs that led to another part of the house.

"Come on," Matt invited. "This is the guest suite."

I've read about houses like that. I've lived lives in books in exactly that sort of house. He opened the door to a dim airless bedroom. It was a large room made small by giant pieces of furniture. He shoved aside heavy drapes and raised a reluctant blind. I went to the window to look out at the view. Through tree branches I could see the tennis court, a gabled boathouse, and in the distance a shimmering curve of lake forming a quiet bay. It took both of us to pry up the window. I leaned on the sill, gazing out, trying to get a breath of fresh air. I pressed my face to the screen. The heat of the sun struggling through the restricting pine boughs reached only as far as the windowsill, unable to penetrate the cool damp-ness of the bedroom. The guest who had reserved the room would last one night. Half the night. And run out screaming at midnight pursued by spooks. And bats. Also spiders.

I had to get out of there because I felt smothered. We went up to Grainger's Ivory Tower, where he hobbled around protecting his leg. He has the whole third floor – bedroom, bathroom, and study, which includes a makeshift kitchen, open windows, and fresh air. We exchanged documents. Grainger claims not to have read mine beyond the first sentence or two, once he realized that it was a personal journal. As if I'd believe that! I know how nosy he is. Also, the fact that he asked me some very pointed questions about Ruth indicates to me that he read all about Ruth's visit on the twenty-fourth of May.

"When is Ruth coming back to visit you?" he asked.

"Who knows?"

"Will she stay here?"

"Couldn't tell you."

"She struck me as a woman of substance."

I'm not at all sure what he meant by that. Probably that she's not an apparition. Anyway, Mrs. Bellington called up eventually, her voice like a silver bell, asking Matt if he would be so kind as to come down to help her.

He didn't come back, and eventually I noticed the time. I told Grainger I had to go and went down to see if Matt could give me a drive home. To the Huddlestons', I mean. At first I didn't see Matt anywhere. I hung around in the hall for a while and then I decided to wait for him in the sitting room. I glanced through the window.

A small car, old but shiny, rounded the curved drive

and stopped. The person in it sat for a moment, got out, surveyed the surrounding area, and, shielding her eyes with her hand against the afternoon sun, looked up at the house. She reached into the car then and hauled out a suitcase. She headed with it up the veranda steps to the front door. There was a pause while she must have tried the useless bell, probably peered through the side windows, and then examined the door knocker. There was a firm *rap-rap-rap* on the door.

I went back out into the hall. Mrs. Bellington appeared, moving with great majesty, scarcely noticing me, and opened the front door. The woman stepped inside. I remembered her. The Elite Cafe, early March. She looked at me with round eyes, as if she wondered where she'd seen me before. She looked at Mrs. Bellington then and said, "It's been a long drive." Her voice was flat. No smile softened her face. She ran a hand through her short sandy-red hair.

"I'm sure you must be tired," Mrs. Bellington said pleasantly. "Let me show you to your room. I thought you might like the same room you had when you were here in March." Matt appeared then, took her suitcase, and told me he would be right down. I watched the woman, followed by Mrs. Bellington and Matt, go up the stairs. "Is that room acceptable?" Mrs. Bellington asked her.

"It doesn't matter," the woman said. "I won't be spending much time in it. I have some detective work to do."

"How do you mean?" I heard Mrs. Bellington ask from the stair landing.

"I made a mistake sixteen years ago. Now I want to rectify it."

I saw Mrs. Bellington turn toward her son, but I couldn't see her face. I could see Matt shrug.

When Matt returned a few minutes later, I was still standing, stonelike, in the same spot. He whispered, "What a weird woman!"

I looked at him and then bulldozed past, striding through the front door, straight down the veranda steps, and across the drive to the winding lane. Matt followed, calling, but I didn't stop. Once out on the highway, I slowed to get my breath and heard a car behind me.

Matt. "What's wrong?" he called through the open car window.

"Nothing."

"I'll drive you home."

"I want to walk."

He stopped and opened the car door.

"Please," I said, bending to look in at him. "I just want to walk." He was looking at me, concerned, looking into each eye, flicking back and forth, as if he could read my mind through my eyes. "Please," I whispered again. I straightened. He closed the car door. I didn't see the car or hear it move, so I guess he sat there watching me.

At the intersection near the Elite Cafe there were signs pointing one way to Wilderness Provincial Park, another way to Ambrose, and another to the Ottawa highway. I had some pretty appealing choices here. I could lose myself in the untamed wilds; I could stay near Ambrose, dug into the Huddlestons' farm; or I could bury my remains in the concrete streets of the city.

I walked quickly along the shoulder. There was an urgency about making up my mind, making a choice. The sun beat down on me, frying my back and arms. The wilderness was inviting. Cool, unpopulated, my sort of place. The holiday traffic was fairly heavy. One car pulling a boat on a trailer and piled high with camping gear went off onto the shoulder, choking me with dust and forcing me into the ditch. I stared after it. All that equipment for roughing it in the wilderness! If I faced reality, I had to admit I wasn't prepared. I didn't even have a match. And even if I had, I wouldn't have the courage to light a campfire.

I could hitchhike to Ottawa, be there in an hour. I went back up to the signpost and turned toward the highway. Cars whizzed past. I put out my thumb, but no one stopped. No one noticed me. Each car looked so private, heading out of the lush countryside for the brick and stone of the city. A speeding car passed me and way up the road squealed its brakes and swerved as it slowed down. I thought it was stopping for me, and I ran to meet it, but it kept going. In the middle of the road lay a mangled porcupine.

I went back to the signpost and aimed my feet for the Huddlestons' farm. And my computer.

The July sun drained away my energy. At the top of a steep hill I moved off the road and into the shade of a cluster of birch trees near a fence. I sat in the middle of a patch of daisies and was rewarded by a small cooling breeze. I removed the clip holding my hair back, shook it free, and leaned back against a fence post to think.

What was I doing, anyway? Running from some strange woman because I think I'm the mistake she made sixteen years ago. I wouldn't even have made the connection if I hadn't happened on that classified ad in *The Globe and Mail*. I can't be the only unclaimed daughter in this county. She has no proof. Her mistake could be three feet tall with green hair for all she knows. There is nothing to link me to her.

I rubbed an arm across my sweaty forehead and tried to think "cool." Chin up and eyes half closed, I looked around, Queen of Cool. A breeze made the daisies bow their heads. I reached out and picked one and then another. I kept picking daisies and then reached out to pick a tall stalk with beautiful blue blossoms growing the length of it. It was one of those flowering weeds you see but don't notice until you look closely. Inside each blue blossom were delicate pink filaments. The flowers were exquisite. When I closed my hand around it, I got a fistful of prickles. Bunch of weeds. I left them there.

It's really late. I should turn this machine off and go to bed, but I won't. I'll tap away until I polish off the whole day.

I got back a little late for supper and then after that we all had to yank weeds out of not only the vegetable garden, but also Ma's flower garden. We pulled long-rooted weeds, short tough clusters of weeds, every kind of weed, plus two runty tomato plants that Ma replanted. We worked until almost dark. When the phone rang and Ma went in to answer it, Hud said we'd call it a day.

"Matt Bellington phoned and said you left an envelope of papers there," Ma said when I went in.

I said, "Oh."

Ma went on and on about Matt Bellington and that he was bringing the papers over and wasn't he an awfully nice lad and blah, blah, and while she was still bleating on about him Matt drove into the driveway. Right behind him, Mrs. Oaksi happened along with a jar of last year's pickles for Ma to sample.

Matt gave me the envelope. I thought he'd leave then, but he didn't. He said, "Can we go someplace and talk?" Good Lord.

Ma and Mrs. Oaksi were in the kitchen yelling at each other about pickle recipes. Ma yells at Mrs. Oaksi because she thinks it helps her to understand English better and Mrs. Oaksi yells back because she's sure Ma's deaf. Hud and the boys were watching the ball game in the living room, so we went outside and into the new room, which now has walls. We squirmed in under the sheets of plastic covering the windows to keep out the weather. The plastic also keeps any existing breeze out and every existing mosquito in.

We sat on the floor and leaned against the wall and slapped at our arms and necks. I waited for Matt to talk. Maybe he was waiting for me. Anyway, no talking was happening, but through the plastic and through the whine of mosquitoes you could hear a whole concert of outdoor sounds. Far in the distance, the sheep settling down for the night murmured their comments out loud. Somewhere out near the apple trees, a whippoorwill stuck on the same three notes but, happy enough with them, whistled on and on. Close by, frogs tuned up for a performance deep in the dewy grass.

"Why were you so upset when you left?" Matt asked. "I can't figure out what I said."

"It wasn't you." In the little bit of light coming from the adjacent kitchen window, I could see how puzzled his eyes were, and how hurt. I shook my head. "Look, you wouldn't understand. Me being upset has nothing to do with you. It's about my life in a world so unrelated to yours that we barely speak the same language."

"I don't understand."

"I told you you wouldn't."

"If you would let me in on it, maybe I would. My life hasn't exactly been a bed of roses, either, you know, I mean, since my father died."

"Oh, right. Knew who he was, though, I guess, did you?"

Matt cleared his throat.

"Forget it. I don't mean to turn this into a contest. That woman reminded me of stuff I'm trying not to think about." We sat for a while in silence, listening to the frogs.

"Grainger told me a bit about you."

"Figured he would. He doesn't know the half of it."

"Tell me."

"I can't. I've forgotten most of it. Everything's vague."

"Like?"

"Once I was afraid of something."

"Of what?"

Thinking about it just then made me wonder if I had mixed up real life with some kind of nightmare I'd had. I thought I remembered unearthly screams and blackness and flashes of hellish light appearing from nowhere, but maybe I didn't. I made myself think of empty spaces, a blank screen. "I can't remember."

He was quiet again. I don't think he's used to quizzing people about their sordid past. He does it so awkwardly. "What can you remember?"

I strained my mind to read something from my past. There was the lady who had given me all the toys. She had wrapped me in her arms and cradled and rocked me nearly to death, crying and crying the whole time. I was always relieved to be put down while the woman poured herself another little "drinky." After that I started school. I loved my grade-one teacher. One day I tried to hug her, but she pushed me away. "I can't be hugging just one child, now can I?" she said. "Why, I'd have to hug the whole class." At first, I thought that would be so nice. Eventually, I came to my senses and saw that it wasn't logical, wasn't possible, that people only like other people in small numbers. What a stupid little kid I was then. I began to play it safe and steer clear of people I might have had an urge to hug.

Don't know what made me dredge that up. "My mind's a blank," I said. The sound of frogs filled the silence between us.

Matt was getting better at quizzing. "What about your real parents?"

"What about them?"

"I mean, don't you wonder about them?"

I concentrated on the frogs. *Cr-a-a-ck, cr-a-a-ck, cr-a-a-ck*, they sang, on and on, into the night.

"Don't you?" he asked again. He had turned to look at me, sitting cross-legged, his elbows on his knees, chin on his knuckles.

I gave in. "Yes."

Br-ea-ea-k, br-ea-ea-k, br-ea-ea-k.

"I hate them." I didn't realize until then that I felt keenly enough to hate.

"Why would you hate them?"

"I hate them for giving me away." I'd never said this before; never even thought it. I don't think I actually hated that woman, the Bellcroft guest, who may or may not be my mother. I hated some mythical, unknowable male and female who, all innocent and unaware, had created me and then changed their minds. Pulled me up by the roots and tossed me out.

"Grainger said they died."

"My adoptive parents died." I wished, then, I could just leave it alone, glue down the lid of my glass box more firmly. I couldn't. Through a crack, bits of me escaped. I blurted, "They abandoned me." I couldn't bear him looking at me, studying me. I got to my feet. "My mother discarded me. Dumped me." I leaned against the frame for one of the windows, pushing aside the sheet of plastic. It fell off onto the floor. A mist rising above the brow of the hill shrouded the tops of the apple trees silhouetted against the pale moon. "Threw out a real live person, a thinking, feeling, hurting person. I hate her!" Matt didn't say anything, but I heard him rustle, stand up. "And what's worse," now I couldn't stop, "what really burns me, is . . . genes."

"Jeans?"

"I've inherited all her rotten genes."

"Oh."

"I'm just like her. Heartless."

"No, you're not."

"What if, through some mistake, I somehow got attached to someone? I'd end up abandoning them, casting them away."

Matt interrupted. "I don't think you would."

He was standing beside me now. We were both looking out at the mist half hiding the moon. "I guess you're right," I said. "I couldn't possibly turn out like my so-called mother. I haven't got anyone to abandon. And never will have. The only thing in this world I'm attached to is my computer. Things have a way of working out for the best, haven't they? I mean, I've spent my life not getting involved with other people, and, for the most part, everyone pretty well leaves me alone. So it works out perfectly. Nobody's a loser."

"You love a machine?"

"Sort of."

"You can't go through life like that."

"Watch me."

I sensed that he *was* watching me. He was silent. Outside, the frogs changed their tune. *F-a-a-ke, f-a-a-ke, f-a-a-ke*, they sang, and in the distance the whippoorwill's mindless refrain continued unchallenged. I said, "Life's a whole lot simpler when you don't need people. As soon as I turn sixteen, I'm leaving here. I can quit school and go up north. Go to the Arctic, if I feel like it. I have no parents to care what I do or don't do. And when I turn eighteen, I won't be a ward anymore. I'll be free. Just me in my own personal paradise."

"Sara." I saw him reach toward me. I felt his hands on my shoulders pulling me close to him. I stood boardlike. I felt his hand in my hair and his shoulder against my cheek. For one brief instant I let myself be aware of how it felt to be me, my soft breasts against his hard chest, and to whiff the faintly damp saltiness of his sweat before I sprang away.

The next instant I glared at him from across the room.

"What did I . . . ? What is it?" he asked. He sounded completely mystified.

"Nothing," I growled. "Why don't you leave?"

"I guess I will, then." His voice was hurt. He slipped out under the plastic sheet covering the spot for the sliding door.

"Pinch me not," I said and I don't care whether he heard me.

I can't help noting, here, that a few months ago, given the same set of circumstances, I probably would have turned into a solid block. Now, I could move, but I didn't feel like it.

Outside the window, the moon was not very big and just hung there, uselessly, partly shrouded in mist. Yesterday I read in the paper that there would be an eclipse this summer, but it wasn't tonight. The moon offered no light. It was not particularly beautiful. Certainly not poetic. I tried, but couldn't even make out a face in it – no man in the moon. I heard Matt drive away. Sometimes I feel that if I cried, I might get a better grip on things. But if I started, would I know how to stop?

I went upstairs and turned on the computer.

Apart from transcribing Grainger's chicken scratches into clearly printed, beautifully punctuated prose, I've avoided this machine for the past week. I've successfully avoided Matt, too, partly because he goes out of his way to avoid me. Yesterday, however, was a disturbing day. I feel compelled to inflict my thoughts on my machine.

Yesterday I worked down at the Ee-lite to help Fran out. The Woman was on her way out just as I got there. I held the door open for her. When she saw me, an expression came over her face that I can only describe as guarded. She looked like somebody trying to play her cards right.

"Nice day," she said to me. It wasn't at all. It was overcast and muggy. I grunted something, I don't remember what.

"That woman!" Fran said after she'd gone. "Enough to give you the heebie-jeebies, isn't she? Looks like she's had all the life sucked out of her."

I put on an apron and didn't say anything.

"She was in here the other day and told me she was looking for her daughter that she'd put up for adoption. That's kind of inneresting, don't you think?"

"Not particularly."

"I thought at first it might've been you."

My heart stopped, then started again. "What do you mean?"

"Well, I mean, she said her daughter was adopted, and I know you're a ward or something of the Children's Aid, which means you're not adopted. I mean, if you're adopted, you're adopted for life, eh? So I didn't mention you to the woman. It wouldn't have been fair to get her hopes up." She looked me in the eye to see if I agreed.

I nodded. I poured more coffee for Ruby McKericher down at the end of the counter. Her sister Pearl hadn't come in yet.

"Too bad, in a way," Ruby said. "Imagine if it was you! Like something you'd see on TV or in a magazine. Long Lost Daughter Found. Now that's exciting." She was giving me a long, intense look, too.

"I don't think it would be very exciting," I said. "Maybe the daughter has plans of her own. Why would she want this woman, who could be a psychopath or anything, messing up her perfectly good future?" Ruby and Fran nodded.

Pearl Hurlehey came in, then. They exchanged a spongy hug before Pearl settled her large behind on the stool beside Ruby. Ruby filled her sister in on the conversation. No paying customer is ever left out of it in this place. Old Vern Dowdle at the other end of the counter was cupping an ear in our direction. A couple of people in the middle stared vacantly into the mirror, not missing a word.

Pearl said, "Oh. Now I know which woman you mean! Course it's exciting. The long-lost daughter would find out she's related to someone. That woman's no psychopath. She's awful thin, though."

Old Vern said, "Don't be too sure about that. There's a lot of it going around."

"Naa, not in these parts there isn't." Tommy Fraderre, a semiregular, was in on it now. "You'd get a lot of it in Toronto, though." He honked his big nose into a handkerchief and dusted its end.

Ruby said, "The long-lost daughter would be just thrilled to find out she had aunts and uncles and grandparents and ancestors." They all beamed their eyes at me now.

"Sisters maybe, too," Pearl added.

I said, "Why would she want them? I wouldn't want relatives, and I couldn't care less about ancestors. Whether I have any or not, I'm still me, alone and glad of it." I pictured myself at that moment, tall, thin, spiky. A sentinel, something like the trees around Bellcroft. Dark. Impenetrable. Evergreens don't send out tendrils. They never have vines attached to them. They stand alone. I looked up from the section of counter I was wiping off and saw them eyeing me like some curiosity you'd see in a glass case.

"You sound just like that woman," Fran said.

"What do you mean?"

"She said to me, 'I never thought I would care much about being related to anyone. I'm a real loner,' she said."

"She said that?"

"And she said, 'I have developed this unexplainable urge to see my baby.'"

"Baby! How old does she figure this daughter is?"

"Sixteen on the thirty-first of August."

I bit the insides of my cheeks and didn't even blink. I bet a hundred and fifty babies were born on the same day as me. I am not necessarily the one.

"She didn't say where she was born, though, did she?" Ruby asked Fran.

They were not all born in the hospital mentioned in the classified ad, however.

"She'll likely tell us. She's in here a lot."

Nor were they all given up for adoption.

"Course she could be an axe-murderer," Old Vern put in.

Which narrows the field.

"Doubt her." Tommy Fradette shook his head.

"We-e-ll, they say you never can tell –"

"Come off it, hardly anybody is."

"– till it's too late."

"Starting to rain," I said, and they all stopped talking

to look over their shoulders at the rain pinging against the window. It came down harder and splashed up from the window ledge.

"Well, the country needs it," Old Vern said.

I went into the back room to wash cups and saucers. I stared at the inside of a cup and thought, they think I'm the daughter. I can tell by the way they keep looking at me. And so does The Woman. But she has no proof, no proof at all. She can't get me unless I agree to be got. I don't have to make any choices until my back's against the wall.

That was yesterday.

It never rains but it pours. (One of Ma's favorite sayings. Among other things.) A little while ago, after supper, I came up here to consult with my machine and only got as far as "my back's against the wall," when I was interrupted by Josh.

"Sara, lemme in!" There was more fear in his voice this time than command.

I hunched over my keyboard. This was becoming a ritual. "Go away, I'm busy!" What I wanted to do just then was work out on my computer how to tell The Woman to crawl back under her rock and how to tell Hud and Ma that I'd be leaving to go north in seven weeks. The information about Timmins came in the mail, so things are shaping up.

Josh continued to bellow and bang on my door. "Oh, for crying out loud!" I gave in. Ma had, after all, asked me

to keep an eye on him and it was getting late, almost dark.
I opened the door.

"Nickie's gonna burn me up!"

"He's not even here. He went somewhere."

"Now he's back."

"He won't hurt you if you stay away from him."

"He will so!" He threw his arms around my hips and
wouldn't let go. I had to pry him loose to take a good look
at him. He stared back at me, his eyes dark with fear.
Something about those eyes struck a chord inside my
chest. From one of those unreachable black caves where I
think my memory lurks, there was a brief flutter. I had a
moment of panic, a memory of fear. Not a specific fear,
just a fear without end, like nightmares I've had that seem
to last forever.

Josh is heavy for four, but I picked him up. First time
in my life I'd ever picked up a little kid. He snuggled right
in and I felt trapped.

"Okay, enough's enough," I growled, and tried to set
him down again on the floor. He clung like a monkey with
both arms and both legs.

"Keep me," pleaded his babyish voice. I don't know
what made him think Nick was going to burn him up.
Nick's the one who'll burn. In hell.

I sighed, gritted my teeth, and struggled down the
stairs and out onto the front porch with this burden.
There was a string-seated rocking chair on the porch,
wobbly but usable. I sat down because the kid weighed a

ton. I rocked a bit while I tried to think of what to do with him. Ma had gone down the road to play cards with some of the neighbors for a little while, but I was under no delusion about that. A marathon talk-fest. Lasting half the night. Hud was down fixing the second gate. Too far to lug Josh. His head bobbed against my cheek as I rocked. His hair felt soft.

I thought I smelled smoke. I managed to tilt Josh's head up to look into his eyes. "Did Nickie really light a fire?"

"Only a little one. In the barn. I snuck out."

Suddenly I was stronger than Josh. I plunked him down on the floor of the porch, ran around the side of the house, and headed for the barn. He began a high-pitched scream. "Don't go!" he cried. "Nickie's gonna burn you!" He ran behind, tripping over his own feet and screaming. And screaming.

I didn't stop. I was propelled toward the barn. I was pulled. Seduced like a sleepwalker into a familiar, recurring dream. At first all I could see was a thin trickle of smoke mingling with the evening mist. My legs pumped steadily, achingly, as I focused on the barn door. Smoke drifted lazily toward me. I knew I was running, but I didn't feel I was getting anywhere. With a poof, like an evil magician's trick, the door was filled with a luminous glow. Beyond, the interior of the barn, cavelike, was half lit. Contrasting shadows danced wildly over the walls.

Josh caught up to me and clutched at my clothes. While he screamed, I stared into the glare until I could stand it no longer. "No!" I yelled. "Stop it! Stop screaming!" I pulled him tight against me and tried to muffle his mouth with my hands. His panic became mine. I staggered back away from the door but lost my footing. Like a three-year-old baby, I sat down hard on the ground. I scraped backward on my seat, digging in and pushing with my heels, trying to get some distance between myself and the blaze.

Once there was a fire.

Memory burst, flooding me, washing over me, wave after black wave. Acrid smell of fear and dying. Maniacal jags of yellow, orange, leaping, receding, closing in upon me.

Josh climbing on top of me, clinging. His screams tearing my eardrums, lacerating my brain. He clutched at me, and I rocked back and forth with him on the ground. Screaming filled my entire existence, became doubled, amplified. My mouth felt stretched; my jaws ached. The screaming was my own.

As magically as it had flared, the fire died. In the barn door Hud appeared, a silhouette, a giant. I heard my screams diminish. They were reduced, finally, to sobs and then gulps of air. I sniffed hard.

Hud set down a huge fire extinguisher and leaned on one arm against the doorframe. He brushed his other arm over his forehead. "Are y'all right?" he called hoarsely, his voice muffled. Josh answered yes for both of us. "I'm okay," I said, then, but I kept on rocking where I sat on the ground, clutching Josh. Hud went to get the hose to wet down the rest of the barn.

With the front of his shirt Josh dabbed at my eyes. "Sara want a Band-Aid?" he crooned into my ear.

I should have felt stupid, embarrassed, to have let myself go like that in front of a little kid like Josh. I slowed my rocking motion and glanced toward the barn. It stood, blackened near the door, but not ruined. You could smell smoke as if someone had lit a campfire. Oddly, I didn't feel stupid for carrying on the way I had. I sat cross-legged on the ground and brushed at my face with both hands. I felt relieved. Or maybe I meant released. Josh squatted in front of me now, looking into my face, his eyes deep not with fear, but with concern.

I stood up and let him hold my hand. I started thinking about Ruth now, and this new feeling I had. Together Josh and I walked to the house. We could hear the swish of the hose water Hud was training into the barn.

If Ruth were to ask me, if Ruth actually wanted to know how I felt at this moment, I would have to say that I felt as though a window, no, a door – a wall had broken down, been blasted out, and fresh air was coming in. Maybe not air, but helium gas, and I was a balloon. I seemed lighter. I would ask her if that was what was meant by a primordial scream. I had read about it somewhere. Later, I thought, I may actually crank out a letter to her. And print it. Even mail it.

It was dark now, and Josh wanted Ma to come home. I said, "No need. It's over now." We stood looking through the kitchen window. To the right loomed the new room; to the left, in the glow from the outside light, we could see

Hud still watering down the barn, giving it a good soaking. The only sound was from the TV droning in the empty living room. Nick was hiding upstairs.

"We need Ma," Josh insisted.

"What for?"

"To talk at us."

I phoned the number Ma had left beside the phone, and Ma said she'd be right home.

"Glory be to Kitty!" she said after surveying the inside of the barn. "Wasn't it lucky the hay's not in yet and only a bale or two left over from last year which is what caught it appears and you happening along when you did Hud and we got that fire extinguisher which we weren't going to get that time but then we did for it saved the barn from a lot of damage."

"There'll be damage done to the seat of Nick's pants, if I have any say in the matter," Hud said. Josh had informed on Nick. "My heart was just a-stepdancin' fit to bust." He went to the bottom of the stairs and hollered for Nick to get himself down here before he had to go up and haul him down by the scruff.

Ma said, "Calm yourself, Hud, sit down, sit down for your own peace of mind and for the boy's sake for he isn't ours and he's a troubled lad and a trouble to us but we need some calming time so we do."

Looking out from under his stringy hair, Nick stood hangdog in front of Hud and Ma Huddleston in the cramped living room. The TV was ominously turned off. When he caught sight of me with Josh, he looked quickly at the floor. I watched proceedings from the doorway, sagging under the weight of Josh, who had clambered back up when Nick came creeping down the stairs. He had his face buried in my shoulder. The room was filled with the sound of Ma's voice for a good five minutes.

"Why'd you do it?" Hud asked at last, after Ma's lecture, which had touched on the general topic of fires, safety precautions, fire escapes, her uncle who was a fireman, and one or two personal experiences related vaguely to fires, all of which seemed to have the effect of diffusing Hud's anger.

"I was just fooling around," Nick said. There was surprised innocence in his voice. He bit his lower lip and looked at Ma. "I didn't mean to."

Josh burrowed deeper into my neck.

"Cigarettes, I s'pose," Hud said.

He looked at Hud now, then turned shame-filled eyes to the floor. "Yes, sir."

Josh turned his head to look at him, but dove back into my shoulder when Nick shot him a warning glance.

"I know I shouldn't have," Nick said to Hud with the voice of someone prepared to take life imprisonment or worse on the chin, if that was what was being handed down. "I found half a pack in the ditch just out by the mailbox."

Ma delivered a lecture on the evils of smoking, listing and describing all the diseases related to smoking along with some that were not.

"Could have burnt the whole farm down," Hud said.

"Coulda burn me all up," Josh offered from the safety of my arms.

"I wasn't going to hurt him. I was getting it out, but then the little crybaby had to run and tell." Nick's voice went back to injured innocence. "I would have got it out. I'm sorry. I guess I just didn't want you to know I was smoking. I went to hide the cigarettes and then . . ."

Josh rolled his head back and forth as if flatly denying Nick's statement and clung even more desperately to me.

Nick looked pleadingly at Ma. I watched him blink his eyes a few times and finally, moisture appeared. "I'm sorry," he whispered.

"Too much free time," reckoned Hud. "Tomorrow I'll line up the chores for you. See if you feel like smokin' after that. Now get on up to bed."

Ma's parting shot at the culprit was, "And no dessert for a week. You hear? A whole week." Nick ran upstairs again, lightly off and knowing it.

Ma noticed Josh in my arms. "What's the matter with him?"

"He's scared of Nick and he's scared of fires. He won't let go."

"Joshy want some chocolate pie?" Ma tempted.

"Yes." Releasing his grip, Josh slid to the floor. He followed Ma out to the kitchen.

"Deserted for dessert." No one heard me. Way of the world, probably.

I went outside to sit by myself on the front porch steps and think about how a primordial scream can make you feel lighter than air. Edith-Ann hauled herself out from under the porch, where she seemed to have taken up residence. She lay on the ground in front of me, alert, panting, her tongue lolling. Tentatively, I reached forward and put out a hand to pat her. From the depths of her soul came a low, guttural warning and I drew back.

Damn dog. Who cares?

I've been away. Ruth phoned me after she got my letter. She said, "Part with some of your hard-earned cash, hop a bus, and come visit me. You need a nonmachine to talk to. I'll treat you to Chinese food."

"Hang on," I said and put my hand over the mouthpiece. I thought I'd better check it out with Ma, who was shaking her head at the radio. "Ma?"

"I know what the temperature is and it's not what the fella on the radio says it is so where's he reading it from upside down or where –"

"Ma?"

"Why I ask you would I be bothered listening to some dope calls himself a weatherman who wouldn't know rain from bathwater and the washing sitting there a mile high not about to do . . ."

"Ma . . ."

". . . itself and the chickens not fed mind you they're laying like nothing on this earth but you can never tell with this new breed we got what's the name of it now oh Hud'll know. Hud?"

"She says it's fine," I said into the phone.

So I went and it was pretty okay. We talked a lot. I took the brochures about beautiful downtown Timmins, but they failed to impress Ruth. "Not as much character as Ambrose," she said. I had to agree, but didn't.

Before I went to visit Ruth, I biked over to Bellcroft to deliver more manuscript pages. I hadn't seen or heard anything of The Woman for a week and wondered if she'd given up and gone away. Her car wasn't in the driveway. Maybe I actually wanted to confront her, to tempt fate. Like running toward the fire in the barn; I couldn't stop myself from running toward the thing I wanted to escape.

The typed pages could have waited, but I also wanted to pick up my pay, which Grainger doesn't always part with willingly. "Sorry," he said. "I keep forgetting."

"Fortunately, I don't."

"Give my regards to Ruth," he said. He's still having trouble with his knee and limps slightly. "Ask her to come and visit us again."

Us? Do I detect a geriatric love affair in the making? Ruth must be pushing forty. And Grainger! Fifty if he's a day. Good Lord.

He didn't come all the way downstairs with me because of his knee. I called good-bye from the second landing and passed the door to the guest wing on my way downstairs.

"Any chance of getting a cup of tea around here?" The Woman was suddenly in the doorway behind me.

I jumped.

She came out onto the stairs. "Sorry," she said. "I thought you were the owner, but you're not, I see."

I gaped at her, trying to recover my wits. I swallowed and tried to say no, but nothing came out.

"Do you know where she is?"

"Wh-wh-who?" My affliction was back.

"The owner. Mrs. Bellington."

"No, s-s-sorry." I continued on down the stairs. The Woman was close on my heels.

"Most disorganized place I've ever stayed in. Of course, that's a small town for you. You'd never get away with this kind of service in Hamilton, where I come from." She pronounced the name "Hamilton" slowly and distinctly.

I stopped in the center of the front hall and took a deep breath. I wanted to close my eyes and disappear. The address listed in the classified ad had been Hamilton.

"I'd b-b-better be going," I said. I opened the door and went outside. The Woman followed.

"Do you know of any other guest houses around here?" she asked my back.

"Nope." I crossed the veranda and went down the steps.

The Woman caught up to me. "I don't really want to look for another place. I can keep my car in the garage here and the house is ideal. It's so cool and comfortable you never want to go outside. I don't think I've ever had a nicer room anywhere. When I close the blind and the drapes, it's just like being in a sealed vault. You feel you could stay in there and nobody'd ever bother you."

I faced her for a brief startled moment before I turned and walked quickly toward the bike.

"Although, I would like a cup of tea now and then," I heard her say.

All the way back I kept my eyes straight ahead. I saw no pink rocks, or fields of daisies, or sheep, or fences. I saw only the road leading on and on. I have given up denying who she is. Up in my room again I was going to indulge in my usual one-sided conversation with my computer, but I didn't. I packed my bag and Hud drove me to the Elite to catch the bus.

I told Ruth about The Woman. She reassured me that I didn't have to do anything against my wishes.

But what *are* my wishes?

Ruth said, "I've never met her in person. What's she like?"

"She isn't like anything. No substance."

"You're beginning to sound like Grainger," she said and added, "which is all right."

Good Lord.

The bus got back to the Ee-lite on a gray Monday morning about ten-thirty. Instead of phoning for Hud or Ma to come and pick me up, I took Pearl Hurlehey's offer of a lift.

"Sure," I said. "Are you going that way, anyway?"

She said, "No, but I don't mind. Save Hud a trip when it looks like rain, and I hear he's getting his hay in."

Josh met me as I was getting my suitcase out of Pearl's car. I waved good-bye as she backed out onto the road. I think I even smiled. When I turned, there was Josh, waggling his fingers beside his eyes at me. "Why are you casting a spell on me?" I asked. "I didn't do anything to you."

"Did so. Went away and left me."

"One night. Big deal."

"So. Maked me throw up, y'know. All over."

"It wasn't my fault. What did Ma let you eat?"

"Nothing. Just bread. And I put some icing on it from the cake and some jam and some brown sugar."

"Right."

"Boy, I hate that."

"Me too."

"Yeah." Josh was taking big steps to keep up to me without running.

In the kitchen Ma was rolling out the daily pie crust. "Home are you," she said, "and did somebody down at the Ee-lite give you a lift likely Ruby or her sister Pearl for they're that goodhearted the two of them and Hud down there in the south field with Nick and young Bellington aiming to get the hay in before it rains and we could certainly use another pair of hands either up here or down there have you had anything at all to eat at Miss Petrie's not that she'd mean to starve you but I sometimes wonder when these working women ever have time to stir a pot for I was a working girl myself at one time when I took the job at Kate's Kozy and Hud he come in there that day and . . ."

"Ma!" I was getting better at blasting through the word barrage. "I'll help. What do you want me to do?"

"I could use you to finish putting together this pie so's I can get on down to help Hud and the lads with the hay before they get dumped on for I don't like the look of that sky even though the fella on the radio said thundershowers later in the day though you can't go by him and keep an eye on Josh too."

I glanced at the flattened-out pie crust and the bowl of strawberries and another ball of dough. I don't know the first thing about making pies. I didn't even know before coming to the Huddlestons' that people actually made their own. "I could help in the field," I said.

"Now there's a thought though I'd never have guessed a town girl would want to drag around on a tractor in the sweat o' the day but it's entirely up to you for I don't mind one way or th'other, Josh you stay up here with me out of the way."

Josh opened his mouth in a loud howl of protest, the noise of which trailed me down almost to the south field, faded and abruptly stopped, probably because Ma plugged his mouth with a big spoonful of glazed strawberries.

Thundershowers arrived later in the day as had been predicted, although not by Ma. Grudgingly she admitted that for once in his life the fella on the radio was right and somebody should mark it on the calendar because it'd be a frosty Friday before it ever happened again.

Standing at the kitchen window watching the rain pelt down, I caught myself smiling, not because of anything Ma was saying, but because of the day I had just spent. Hud taught me to drive the tractor.

It was a terrifying experience at the start, but after grinding the gears a few times and jolting the thing like a bucking bronco, I managed to get the hang of it. I liked tottering along, bracing myself as the machine jostled over uneven ground. Hitched to the tractor was the baler, trailing along the windrows where hay had been gathered into long lanes.

I seemed to be standing away from myself, watching the whole operation as if it were a movie. We were surrounded by a field of green and yellow and brown with a slate sky hanging over the whole scene like a threat.

A rising wind shuffled through the windbreak of poplars at the edge of the field. Their leaves shimmered from green to silver and back to green. The baling machine gobbled its way along the rows of hay, magically depositing heavy, rectangular eggs as it went. Nick dragged the bales out of the way of the machine. Hud and Matt hoisted and stacked them into lopsided pyramids, which would give them some protection from the coming rain.

Matt, so far, hadn't looked up from his work. I felt invisible. So I turned him invisible, too.

Nick's nose was out of joint because he couldn't drive the tractor. "Next summer," Hud said. "A little more weight and a little more height and there'll be no holding you back. You'll be flyin' rockets to the moon, more than likely."

Nick didn't say anything. He gave me a sour look that took in my whole anatomy. He had a habit, when Hud wasn't looking, of letting his eyes linger on the front of my tee shirt. When I turned my back on him, he hissed a tight laugh through his teeth. He knows how to control people. I'll be long gone from this place when he finally starts to grow. For the time being, and with Hud never far away, he's more of a nuisance than a menace.

Long gone, I thought single-mindedly, bumping along with the big steering wheel in my hands. Alone. I heard a distant rumble of thunder. I turned the corner of the field in a wide sweep, and just for a moment, field and sky looked fused into one lifeless shade of yellowing gray. I looked down. In front of the tractor a brown rabbit crouched, petrified, frozen in the act of choosing a direction.

I somehow let the engine stall. With a flash of white tail, the rabbit bounded away and down his lonely hole.

"What's wrong?" Hud was calling from a ridge where the land swept uphill. He was braced with his legs wide, his hands on his hips, only the sky behind him. He reminded me of a picture of Atlas I saw once in a book of Greek myths. He looked as if he could shoulder the world if he had to.

"Stalled," I said. I tried the starter, but it didn't catch. The engine groaned. Matt straightened his back and looked over at me.

"Ease up on the gas," Hud called.

"It's flooded," Matt said over the engine's whine.

We let it sit for a while, watching the wind sweep in gusts through the windrows. Hud sent Nick to bring the sheep up. I looked up the slope and then back over the field we'd already covered, surveying the day's accomplishment.

I said, "I like this kind of work. You can see where you're going and you can see where you've been."

"Making your mark on the land." Hud had come over to where I was sitting on the tractor and looked at me with that relaxed smile he has. "Chip off the old block," he said, just as if I was related to him. "The thing about land is, it's there." Matt was resting, sitting on a boulder that had probably been there since the last ice age. His eyes were on Hud as if he thought he was the prophet Isaiah. "There's some that figure land is what you own, or else something you scrape off your boots, or maybe frame and hang on a wall. But it's what you work. It's what binds body to soul. Here," he said, "let me have a go at that engine."

"No, wait," I said. "Let me try again."

"Use your ears, then," Hud said. "She's a temperamental old beast. Listen for it. When she's just about ready, give her the choke, but don't let her cough herself dry. Understand?"

"Yep." The machine roared into action and I looked up at Hud.

"You're the girl!" he said. "Knows her machines, this one," he said to Matt. I took a quick look in Matt's direction before I put the tractor in gear. I think I saw the corner of his mouth turn up in what you might call a wry smile. He was probably thinking about my attachment to my computer. Anyway, the smile softened his face. I bumped into action and had to look straight ahead to watch where I was going.

Standing there at the kitchen window, watching as the rain began to slow up, I could see the reflection of my smile. I watched it fade as I thought about what had followed the tractor episode.

We came up from the field when it started to rain. Hud invited Matt in to wait out the worst of it, and Ma gave everybody a mug of tea at the kitchen table. She took a lemon loaf out of the oven and made us eat a slice of that. Two slices. Somehow it ended up just Matt and me left alone in the kitchen. Nick never hangs around Matt. He went upstairs. Ma started rushing around to clear up the dishes because her TV program was on and I said, "Leave them, I'll do it."

Her mouth dropped open a little because I don't usually offer to do things for people. Matt hadn't finished. Thunder rumbled. Hud went out to the barn with Josh hot on his heels. "He has to tuck the sheep in so they won't be afraid of the storm," I said just for something to say.

Matt continued to sit at the table, scraping at a callus on the palm of his hand. His glasses sat on the table in front of him. I began to remove his cup. "Are you finished?"

"Yes, let me help you." He started clearing the table.

"You don't have to." I picked up the cake plate.

"It doesn't matter." He started to take the dishes from me. I didn't want him helping me in this cramped kitchen, so close to me. I hung on to the empty cake plate, but he didn't let go. I looked up, embarrassed, angry at my embarrassment.

"I don't *need* help."

"I don't mind." He smelled of hay and sweat and tractor grease. Without his glasses on he looked like an explorer contemplating new and dangerous land.

I hate seeing people look vulnerable. I feel like telling them to get a grip. I said, "Are you deaf?"

He let go of the plate and I nearly dropped it. He put his hand out to steady it and accidentally touched my hand. I stared down at his arm, his wrist, and felt ashamed of the anger in my voice.

Matt backed away. I thought he was about to say something, but instead he closed his mouth and scratched his head. He looked at the floor as though he had found something there that he didn't understand.

"Well, all right," I muttered, "we'll both clean up if you like."

He shrugged, wary, and then nodded.

I threw him the damp dishcloth. "Here, you can wipe off."

He scrubbed at the table, sticky and smudged where Josh had sat. I was rinsing stuff under the tap. When I turned it off, he said, "Why are you always so angry with me?"

I put the mugs in the dishwasher. "I'm not always angry with you. I hardly know you."

"You make me feel as if . . . as if I don't quite measure up. Do you hate me?"

"I never hate people." I turned on the tap again to soak a spoon. "I'm neutral about everybody. My life is kind of uncertain," I said over the rush of the water, "unpredictable, so I can't afford to spend much time . . . getting to know people."

"Why not?"

"They keep disappearing." I was turning red, like something newly peeled. I packaged up the rest of the lemon loaf and covered the butter.

He turned off the tap. "I'm not going to disappear."

"You might. You don't know for sure."

"Why don't you take the chance that I won't?"

"I don't take chances. That's what I'm trying to avoid, that's why I make plans. I just want to move from A to B. No hitches. No entanglements." I was running out of things to do. I shoved the milk into the fridge and closed it. I had my back to the fridge door. "I used to be able to blank people out whenever I wanted."

"Can you blank me out?" He stood near the table and rubbed his eyes. He put his glasses on. He was looking at me, curious, involved. That can be so unnerving.

I looked away. I bent over the dishwasher and rearranged the cups. My neck and cheeks felt as if they'd been boiled.

"Can you?"

"Not sure. I haven't figured out what type you are yet."

"Type?" He was beginning to sound a little hurt. "You categorize people into types? What are you doing? Compiling an encyclopedia?"

"Not exactly. Some types I can forget easily, some take longer."

"You can't make a type out of me. I'm an individual."

This was more like it. An argument, harsh words, and

bingo, he's gone. I shook my hair out of its tie-back to let it stand out in an angry blaze. "An individual what?" I wanted sarcasm to flow lavalike into the cool space between us. "You're specimen A," I said with as much contempt as I could.

He didn't look angry, he looked hurt.

"Come on," I jeered, "don't tell me you didn't type me, because I know you did."

Matt stared hard at me, thinking, then turned to look through the window. Rain was starting to come in. He shoved his hands deep into his pockets and hunched up his shoulders. "Maybe."

"Right. How did you categorize me?"

"I don't know." He was still looking out the window.

"What did you think I was like?"

He turned around and looked at me. "A woman to be reckoned with."

"A woman –"

He nodded.

"To be reckoned with?"

He nodded again.

"What does that mean?"

"Someone who knows where she's going, I guess, and knows how to get there."

I thought of my cool, clear north, of the brochures about Timmins listing its shopping malls, hockey arenas, churches, schools. I thought of the map I have of northern Ontario and the way it runs out of red highway lines once you get up beyond Moose Factory. And I thought, this guy doesn't even know where I'm headed and yet he thinks I know how to get there. I felt a tiny moment of panic, as if I had managed to fool everybody but myself. That was stupid, though, because I *was* going north and *could* find my way without any difficulty whatsoever. "I'm going away at the end of August," I said. "And I know where and how."

He came over and closed the door of the dishwasher. I think I was rearranging the dishes for the third time. "Why would you want to do that?" he asked.

I was forced to look directly into his face. "Because I'm dropping out. I have bad luck with foster homes." He was standing inches from me. I had a brief memory of the panic-stricken rabbit in front of the tractor, not knowing which way to turn. The dishwasher was in my way; Matt was in my way. Something powerful was bearing down on me. He reached out toward my hair. It took all my willpower to stand still, not to bash his hand away. I must have *wanted* him to touch my hair. He tucked a strand of it behind my ear. I felt my eyes moving back and forth as I stared into his eyes. His knuckles brushed my cheek.

I bit my lip because I thought he was looking at my mouth. Through the window I saw lightning split the clouds. The thunder cracked, rattling the sky or possibly my brain. I couldn't handle any more. I must have looked panicky. He stepped back.

I noticed the way his Adam's apple moved up and down. So unprotected. What if I had leaned forward and kissed it?

Good Lord.

He said, "I'd better go."

"You'll get drenched."

"I have Grainger's car."

I watched him reach out and open the door to outside.

"Sara?" Ma calling from the living room. "Can you help me get this window closed I swear it grows half an inch every year. Sara?"

"Coming."

Matt was looking at me. "I'm going, but I'm not disappearing," he said. "I'm the type that doesn't disappear." Then he went out. Through the window I watched the rain envelop him like a sheet. He tilted his head up, drinking rainwater. He turned around and walked backward toward the car, grinning, watching me watch him. He drove away into the lightning.

Rain slanted through the open kitchen window, and all I could think about was Matthew Bellington's Adam's apple moving up and down and the black hair, so appealing, on the backs of his elegant wrists. Good Lord. An emotional marshmallow.

I closed the kitchen window.

"Sara?"

"Coming."

Good Lord.

The rain was far from over, but the wind had died. I shoved up the kitchen window again and filled my lungs with the sweet hay smell and the rich pungency of earth. I had the peculiar sensation of being in the center of something, maybe the universe. Josh and Hud were back from comforting the sheep. Thunder rolled overhead. In the distance lightning lit the glowering sky, and all around the little box-house the rain beat down as if once having got started, it couldn't stop. A talk show Ma had no use for chattered from the living room, and the drone of Hud reading to Josh at the kitchen table lent a mingling, melting effect to this whole sensation I was experiencing. Not even Nick could spoil it. He was nowhere to be seen. Upstairs still, I guessed. I heard him come down, then. He stood smirking at me in the kitchen doorway, and my feeling of being in the midst of something universal began to fall apart.

I could hear the television. Nick went into the living room, and I moved away from the sound to sit at the table.

"We read gas barbecues already," Hud said to Josh. "What about wheelbarrows?"

"I hate wheelbarrows," Josh said, flipping pages of the catalog and scanning them for more passionate items to excite his imagination.

Hud looked up at me with dog-tired eyes over reading glasses perched on the end of his nose and shook his head. "Starts school in the fall. What the teacher'll make of him I'll never tell you. Never even heard tell of Humpty Dumpty and all them. Thinks Sleeping Beauty's a kind of grass seed."

The rain continued off and on for several days. Hud got a well-earned rest and looked the better for it. I went into town with him in the truck to get supplies. "Sixteen soon, aren't you?"

I nodded.

"Get you drivin' the truck soon's you turn."

I smiled. But then I stopped smiling because I wouldn't be here long enough to learn. The minute I turn sixteen I'm packing my bag.

"When I turn sixteen, I can leave," I told Hud.

He looked across the seat toward me and then turned his attention back to the road. "That's true enough, I s'pose." When I next looked at him, I thought his face had a hurt look. He looked like Josh after I'd pinched him.

I looked straight ahead at the road, too.

CHAPTER
8

*I*t's nearly the end of July. I'm now helping Fran out at the cafe not only on Wednesdays and Saturdays, but also noon hours nearly every day.

Yesterday The Woman came in for lunch and sat at a table near the window. I wanted to hide under the counter. Old Vern was the only one of the regulars there, and he was just getting his wallet out of his pocket to pay his bill. Fran had gone into town to the post office, so I couldn't escape. There were a couple of other people, but they were busy talking to each other, not interested in anyone else.

I brought her the menu.

"I'm still here," she said. "I only booked the first two weeks in July at that B and B, but I've decided to stay on for a bit." She was staring right into my eyes. "You know, I came to this area to locate my daughter."

I made some sort of strangled sound and went back to the cash register. Old Vern paid. I handed him his change and he left. I went back to The Woman to take her order.

She said she'd have the beef stew and I nodded, intending to disappear into the back room until I'd heated up a plateful for her. "You see, I had a child," she said to my back. "Have a child," she corrected herself. "I had to give her up for adoption, and now I want to see her, to meet her." Her voice was high pitched, eager.

I had every intention of ignoring her, of getting on with my job, but I heard myself asking, "Why?" Without even stuttering. Is this what they mean by the human condition, that this is what we do? We run headlong to meet our fate? I even turned and looked at her.

The Woman said, "Why do I want to meet her? I guess it started as a whim, really, but now it's something more than that. It's becoming more like an obsession. Maybe I made a mistake. Maybe I shouldn't have given up my baby." Her eyes were shining and the skin around them looked taut. Her face was becoming mottled.

I went back to the counter. The other people paid and got up to leave. I went into the back room and came out again, presently, with The Woman's stew. She sat there, silent now, filling space with her presence, looming, looking every so often in my direction. She dawdled over her meal, separating the carrots out of it and lining them up along the edge of her plate. I wanted her to go.

"You live on a farm near here, I understand."

I said, "Yes."

"You're almost sixteen, aren't you? Old enough to quit school if you want."

I took a breath.

"I'd like my coffee warmed up," she said.

I filled The Woman's coffee cup. She reached out as if she would touch my arm, but stopped when I jerked away.

"I want to find her, just to talk, you know." She was almost whispering now. "I never did get married. I don't have anyone else, except an old aunt I look after. When she goes, I'll have no one."

I put the coffee pot back on the burner and heard her stirring in sugar.

She started up again, louder and more rapidly, as if she'd memorized a sales pitch and wanted to get it all in before she lost her audience. "It's a nice life we have right now, just the two of us. We have a factory, well, a small factory, where we make imitation flowers, mostly out of fabric, but some out of plastic. Aunt Bella's beyond it now, of course. I have to hire people to help me. It's a good business. We sell to stores, and people come right to the factory, too, to buy the plastic ones. I've noticed people like to buy them to put on graves. They last forever, although we've had complaints that the sun bleaches out the colors. They should buy white. That's what I tell them."

I had my back to her, wiping a smudge off the mirror. I tried to wipe away the reflection of her face beaming hopefulness at me, but failed. Fran had come in through the back door. I could hear her rearranging cans and jars on the shelf. I hoped she would come and rescue me.

The Woman continued to stick-handle her stew around

on her plate. "Straightforward business," she said. "On-the-job training. You don't need much education to run it. You need to know how to add and to read. That's all. In fact, knowing a lot of the useless frills they teach you nowadays would be a handicap. I mean, how many times a day do you think about dinosaurs? Who cares why they became extinct?"

I didn't think she had a point, but I didn't want to get involved. I rinsed out my cloth.

"Mind you," she went on, "I haven't always been in the imitation-flower business. I used to be a schoolteacher, but I gave that up."

I should have gone then to join Fran in the back room, but instead I asked The Woman why she had given up teaching.

"Kids. Couldn't stand them. Day in, day out, these pestering kids always wanting you to pay attention to them, to listen to them, anything to get out of just sitting there learning to add or to read. I couldn't take that kind of nonsense. So I quit." She stirred her coffee again, banged the spoon on the edge of her cup, and clunked it onto the saucer.

"Became a receptionist in a dentist's office then. It wasn't too bad, except for the patients." I was looking right at her now, fascinated. "You'd always have to be so nice and polite to them, and they didn't appreciate the fact that you were going out of your way to do so. All they could think about was their teeth and what the dentist was going to do to them."

She saw that she had my full attention and raced away with it. "So then I went in with my aunt making imitation flowers, and it suits me just fine. We live right down in an area where there are lots of factories and small businesses and so forth. No grass to cut, which is nice. Not many neighbors, either, which can be a blessing. Oh, we're happy enough."

I had been staring, compelled to stare, directly into The Woman's eyes. She sipped her coffee and gazed back. I had to escape. I picked up two empty glasses and headed with them into the back.

"I just wondered –" The Woman called and paused. With my back to her, I waited for her to go on. "I mean, I understand my daughter is free to choose."

I felt my heart thud inside my chest. I thought about the black paper heart hidden in my drawer at the Huddlestons' and wanted to scream, "Too late!" Slowly, I turned and looked at her, wondering if I could control my voice enough to tell her.

She kept on talking. "And I just thought, well, if she knew what a nice life we'd have together, she'd feel easier. What she'd have is money. I don't spend a lot, so I've got a lot. Enough, anyway. Never been in debt to anyone in my life. And of course she'd have a lot of freedom. I wouldn't get in her way. I believe in privacy. I leave the world alone, and it pretty well ignores me. She'd be independent, running the factory by the time she was eighteen. Set for life."

I put the glasses back down on the counter and looked The Woman in the face.

She continued, "I don't suppose it's the fanciest place to live, but it suits me. Above the factory I look out my window onto a sea of slate-colored roofs. Below it's like a gridwork – cool, gray concrete streets and square, black parking lots. It's uniform and it's peaceful."

We stared at each other. She was waiting for me to say something, looking at me with the only emotion I'd ever seen on her face. Hope.

My voice had gone on an extended vacation.

The Woman shoved her plate away. I rang up her bill.

She gave a tired sigh. "I was hoping she'd want to go back with me soon. I don't like to leave Aunt Bella too long." She paid her bill, looked carefully around the cafe as if she expected to find two or three potential daughters skulking about in the corners, and left, letting the screen door slam behind her.

Ruth's coming next week for Civic Holiday weekend, and will be curious to know more about how I feel about this woman – with her privacy, and her imitation-flower factory. And her money. The bribe of a desperate woman, I guess. I keep seeing her eyes. Those needy eyes. I don't know . . . She's a bit sad. A bit of a sad case. I wish I could hate her.

If it's not one thing it's about five hundred others, as Ma says. Now it turns out that Josh's mother is going to put in an appearance. Ma's afraid she'll want to take the little blister back. When she told me this, I was going to say, let her. Who cares? But I didn't. Ma looked so completely heartbroken.

I'm in danger of turning to slush.

I started looking around at all of them. I got to thinking about one of those puzzle books I used to have when I was little with a page in it that asked what's wrong with this picture? Hud and Ma and Josh and everybody all looked as if they went together perfectly, and if one was missing, then there would be something wrong with the picture. I would never tell anyone that, with the possible exception of Ruth, if she started trying to probe the depths of my psyche. At the time, we were outside near where Hud's building the new room. Ma was cutting Josh's hair with her sewing scissors and saying they'll never be the same again.

I said, "Josh's head'll never be the same again."

Josh, who had a little hand mirror, said, "I hate this kind of haircut."

"What kind do you want?" I asked him.

"Long and curly." He was studying mine.

"I'll see what I can do," Ma said.

We could hardly hear ourselves think because Hud and Matt were hammering nails into the roof. Matt is in seventh heaven. He spent half an hour yesterday afternoon describing to me in minute detail how to shingle a roof. Born to instruct. I said "Mmm," and "Well," and "Mmm" quite often during his dissertation and thought about Josh's mother coming and whether or not I would miss him if he went away. I didn't reach a definite conclusion.

Nick was given the job of taking a sledgehammer and knocking the bricks out of the wall of the kitchen next to the new room. He's turning a window into a door. It's the only job he's ever liked doing. We decided to stay outside until he's finished. I think Ma and I both had visions of the place crumbling around our ears if he got a notion to take a swing at a bearing wall. The mosquitoes are still pretty thick. Ma and I want to get one of those tent gazebo things.

Well, it happened. About Josh, I mean, not the house falling down. Actually, it's just as if the house had fallen down. Josh's mother and her boyfriend pulled into the driveway in an ancient minivan that's seen better days. Josh was kind of excited at first because he had forgotten what his mother looked like. Shopworn would describe her. She handed him a bag containing three store-bought chocolate eclairs, which went a long way toward breaking the ice. Ma looked at the whipped cream with a certain degree of suspicion. "The Lord only knows how long that's been sitting around in this heat," she said to me. It wasn't until Josh was inside the van, all stuffed and sticky, that he realized what was happening.

They drove away with Josh screaming blue bloody murder and trying to climb out through the window. I stood there watching and feeling my throat get so tight I couldn't swallow. At least I have a choice about whether I go with my mother. I bet they gave him a good swat once they were out of sight. They looked like the type.

I stood watching the dust raised by the car and felt little pinpricks behind my eyes. I had to keep blinking.

Things sound kind of hollow around here, as if there's going to be an echo. I've been working very hard on Grainger's manuscript. The reason I can get so much typing done is because there are no more interruptions. Josh's cats are noisy. They probably miss him. Edith-Ann goes around with a kind of hangdog look, but then, she normally does. Of course, I'm used to a lot of changes going on in my life, so I can handle it. Although I didn't think it would be this quiet. Ma hardly opens her mouth anymore. I asked what the weather was supposed to be today and she said she didn't know. I asked her what the fella on the radio had said and she said, "Who?" Hud looks old.

Nick's happy. He goes around whistling. I'd like to belt him one. I think he'd like to be an only child.

I've been leafing through the Canadian Tire catalog and found a section on kerosene heaters I bet Josh would have liked. Not that it matters. Anyway, who cares? Matt says I act depressed, but I'm not. Why would I be? Hud told Ma she should go over and talk to Mrs. Oaksi, but she didn't want to. This is so incredibly boring. I have nothing to say. Matt asked me to go with him to a movie in Ambrose, but I said no. I've already told him I don't get involved with people. I don't know why he doesn't disappear.

Fran didn't need me yesterday or today, so I've been stuck here. Today I delivered some typed pages to Grainger. His knee is better, and he said he'd come pick them up, but I needed to escape this house of gloom. Grainger's been going around interviewing people in the area, getting some authenticity into his book. Does he actually expect anyone to take it seriously? He's got Ruby's and Pearl's Grandma Cooch in. When I got there, he was just getting into his car to go talk to Vern about the Dowdle family's witch. "Witch!" I said. "Aren't you mixing your metaphors here?"

"Don't be such a spoilsport," he said. "Vern's great-aunt's aunt on his mother's side had the second sight, as they say. She was very well known in the area, although she lived a few miles south of here. People used to come from miles around, by horse and buggy, to have their fortunes told. It's been said that even Sir John A. Macdonald availed himself of her services."

"So how does she like hobnobbing with ghosts in your book?"

"She comes back, now and again, apparently."

Standing there in the driveway, I just shook my head. I looked up at the shadowy old house and said, "Bellcroft. Good name. The place is full of ding-a-lings." Grainger just laughed and got into his car. He rolled down the window and stuck his head out. "Nobody's forcing you to believe in ghosts. But remember, if somebody sees a ghost, ghosts exist. For somebody." He drove away and I could see him watching me in the rearview mirror.

The Woman came around the corner of the house as I was leaving. "Oh, it's you, is it?" she called. I kept on going toward the tree where my bike was propped. I looked back and saw that she was following me. She had to skirt the low-hanging dead branch of one of the sentinel trees. It snagged her sandy-red hair as if trying to pull her back, but she broke it off and quickly caught up. She began talking to me as if this were simply a continuation of the conversation we'd had at the Elite at the beginning of the week. "I'll have to get back to the factory soon. You see, I have one of the hired girls come to look in on Aunt Bella, but she'll want her vacation. This is our slack time, of course, with everything in bloom, although why anyone would want real flowers, I couldn't tell you. They just die."

I ducked through the weeping willow's curtain of foliage, leaving The Woman standing in the drive. "You have lovely hair," she said.

I wrenched my bike away from the tree and into the driveway. The Woman reached out and placed a hand on the handlebar. I was forced to stop. I felt myself staring into her round eyes.

She said, "Mine was never that thick."

I looked down at her hand preventing me from moving my bicycle. "I have to go," I said.

"Oh yes, certainly. Sorry." She took her hand away but kept talking. "I want my baby back. I suppose I shouldn't, but I tend to think of her as a baby. I think she'd be enough like me that she'd really like the factory. There are

worse things than making imitation flowers for a living."
She gave me a long look.

"I have to leave," I said again. I pushed down on the
pedal and strained uphill along the rutted lane. Before I
reached the first twist in the drive, I looked back over my
shoulder. The Woman was still planted in the middle of
the lane. A question of sorts formed in my mind. I stopped,
hesitating about whether or not to ask it. Perhaps it should
have been reserved for my computer and not hung up in
the air between us like so much laundry. But I wanted an
actual response, which, so far, my computer has been
incapable of providing.

I scraped the bike halfway around and called out to
The Woman, "Maybe the baby turned out to be like its
father."

She walked toward me. "The father! Don't make me
laugh. I don't know where he is now, and I don't want to.
One of these brainy types, you know? Oh, he left me fast
enough. He's gone on to higher things by now, I expect.
An absentminded professor or a mad scientist, I should
think. Who needs him? Who wants him? For my baby's
sake, I hope she isn't like him."

I got on the bike and left. I shouldn't have asked.

As soon as Ma finishes her inside work she goes outside to
shovel manure or load hay bales onto the wagon. She never
stops and she hardly ever says a word. Hud never stops
working, either, he and Matt. If they're not out with the
sheep or down in a field, they're working on the addition.

The windows are in, lots of them, but we haven't started to use the new room yet. Mrs. Oaksi's nephew came to help Hud plaster the walls in return for the promise of a sack of potatoes and a basket of apples.

The room has a character all its own, even though it's supposed to be part of the house, a kind of extension of the kitchen. A family room, Hud calls it. Josh would have liked all the windows. I offered to paint the woodwork.

"What color?" Hud asked.

I ran my hand over the light pine framing the windows, sanded smooth and rounded at the edges, Matt's work. I gazed beyond the east window to the old maple near the corner of the house, a flush of pink already touching some of its leaves. To the south, the first three of Hud's apple trees, dotted with ripening fruit, crowned the hill as it sloped gently toward the cornfield. The west window was actually the sliding glass door. From here you could step out and almost be in the midst of Ma's flower garden. I didn't know the names of the tall blooms whose colors spanned the rainbow, or of the bobbing heads of shaggy-petaled blossoms that seemed to drink in the sun and then reflect it. I just knew that the flowers lent vibrance to the new room.

"There's such a thing as clear paint, isn't there, no color?"

"Yep," Hud said.

"Then that's what we need for the wood."

The plaster had dried to a gleaming white. I got Ma to look at it in the soft light of early morning. She had been thinking of wallpaper splotched with stylized jungle flowers but closed the sample book and put it away. "White is nice," she said. The background of green through the windows arced by blue haze was decoration enough. On the floor was a rush mat. Someone had once given it to Ma, she couldn't remember who. She'd never given it much thought and had kept it rolled up and stored in the shed. Beaten and wiped down and hung out to air, it lay now on the wood floor like a carpet of new-mown hay.

Nick's going around all cheerful and mysterious. Sometimes I see him just staring at me.

I've been helping with the sheep just to escape Ma's sad eyes. The sheep are noisy and smelly but not as stupid as they look. Hud calls them up to their pen by rattling a pail of oats, and they come trotting up the hill on their dainty feet, as tame as can be. He has a lot of patience with them. Hud's the kind of person who would have invented sheep if they hadn't been thought up already. There's one small black one Josh would have chosen to keep in his room.

We found another hole in the fence, and a sheep got through. The fence may have been rotten, but it looked to me as if somebody had broken it with a big rock.

"Nick, probably," I said.

Hud said, "Maybe. Should be spending more time with him, I guess, to keep things from going wrong. He seems to need a person's undivided attention."

The escaped sheep had fallen into a gully and ended up on its back (cast is the word Hud used) and couldn't get out, so Hud and I had to give it a boost. Hud said we saved its life because it can't breathe properly on its back. I was up to my ankles in sheep shit for the second time in my life before the ordeal was over. Not a pleasant sensation. Making plastic flowers for graves is beginning to have a certain appeal. Hud said I was a grand lass.

I think Nick goes through my stuff when I'm out helping Hud. I took ten dollars out of my hiding spot and put it in my desk drawer. If it disappears, I'll know. I thought I heard Josh hollering just now, but it was just the TV. I'm pressing exit. This machine is boring.

At ten after ten on the Friday morning of Civic Holiday weekend, the beginning of August, the phone rang. Ma and I, both up to our elbows in flour, looked at each other. I had asked for a lesson in pie-making, thinking it might give Ma something to talk about, and was in the process of re-rolling out my third moth-eaten crust. Ma said, "I'll get it," and wiped her hands on the dish cloth. "Moses 'n' Aaron!" she said after listening into the phone. "Ah, the poor wee soul." I put down the rolling pin, to hear better. "Well, wouldn't we just! Of course, of course! Bring him on out for we haven't changed a thing even his bed's in the same place and the side that goes up too so he won't fall out not that he's needed it this past six months for he's got to be such a big lad and all pardon? Oh, not at all that's just fine whenever you get here we'll just be that happy to have him back tell him . . . Hello? Oh. Well now." She put down the phone. "You'll never guess what," she said.

I took a long-shot guess, hummed a little tune, and rolled out a perfect crust. Ma went outside to find Hud and Nick to tell them and then she got on the phone to Mrs. Oaksi. I had to put the rest of the pie together partly by guess and by gosh and partly through Ma's attempts at sign language while she spent the next twenty minutes loudly telling Mrs. Oaksi that Josh was about to return to the fold.

Later in the day, the car bearing Josh pulled into the driveway. He scrambled out, slammed the car door, and plunked himself down on the grass with his eyebrows bunched together and his mouth knotted up. He started pulling up grass and spreading it over his knees as if it were a blanket and he was tucking himself in. He had a black eye.

"What's the matter?" Hud said. "Aren't you glad to be back?"

Josh said, "I shoulda never went."

Ma went to him with a stream of low, cuddly words and put her hand on his head, but he shied away and tried to sink lower into the grass. Hud said, "Leave him be for a bit. He'll come round." The social worker who had driven him out asked to have a private word with the Huddlestons and they went inside. Nick, who had been in a bad mood ever since the morning's phone call, wasn't around.

I sat on the grass in front of Josh. He kept on pulling tufts of grass out by the roots, not looking at me. I looked at the car parked in the driveway behind him. I pressed my fists into my temples and started wagging both index fingers at the car. Josh looked up through his eyebrows, his mouth still in a tight knot. He looked over his shoulder at the car. It was still there. He ducked his head back down. After a while the social worker came outside. I felt stupid, but I kept on casting my spell. The social worker stared at me with slightly raised eyebrows but called good-bye to Josh. He turned to look at her and watched her get into the car, watched as she sat there turning the key in the ignition. Slowly he turned himself around, brought his fists to the sides of his head and wriggled his fingers at her. The social worker bit her lip, frowned a little, and backed quickly out of the drive. Josh jumped up and yelled, "Pinch me not!" at the departing cloud of dust. He went inside then to ask Ma what was for supper.

Josh didn't have much to say during supper about his sojourn with his mother, so no one pressed him. Just before the end of the meal he looked around the table and said, "She punched m' lights out. See?" He pointed to his black eye. Ma made a tsk-tsking sound and put another piece of pie on his plate.

"What did you do to her?" I asked.

"Nothin'."

"Yeah, right."

"Kicked over her can of beer," he admitted, finally. "And threw another one. Threw another one right through the window."

I nodded. Hud cleared his throat.

Nick stared hard at Josh. "Did you break the window?"

"Yes!" Josh sounded surprised that he even had to ask.

We were all looking at him now. He said, "They were yelling and fighting and everything, and I hate that!" He meant it. When I looked at him now, I saw a boy, not a baby. I know what he's been through. Nick eyed him, considered him, his mouth skewed to one side as if he detected something rotten, as if his life were spoiled.

Ma and I were scraping the plates and rinsing them and loading them into the dishwasher. Ma said that the fella on the radio said there would be an eclipse of the moon tomorrow night and we should all stay up to watch it unless we fell asleep first. I said that I'd watch it for sure and wouldn't fall asleep and what had the social worker said about Josh? I'm beginning to wonder if Ma's habit of running all her thoughts together is catching for maybe it is. Then Ma described in point-by-point detail what the social worker had said about Josh's mother who didn't want him after all and as far as she was concerned he could be put up for adoption and it'd serve him right that's what the mother said and –

Josh careered into the kitchen. "Something's wrong with Hud out in the barn!" he shrieked.

Ma stopped midsentence and shot out to the barn with me close behind and Josh bobbing along telling me to wait up. In the dust-specked shaft of early evening light slanting through the barn door we saw Hud pick himself up off the floor and sit heavily on a wooden box. His face looked bleached out and was beaded with sweat. "Just a weak turn I took," he said to Ma, who stood over him hands on her hips. "I was bawlin' out Nick," he said by way of explanation.

"What'd he do?"

"Not much. Teasin' the cat."

"And you got yourself all worked up over –"

"He had a length or two of twine –"

"And you gave yourself a weak turn about –"

"One end 'round the cat's neck and –"

"I'm marchin' you right into town to the doctor's and –"

"Th'other over that rafter. I come in just in –"

"Sara, you look after Josh, I'm takin' Hud in to see Dr. Cornish, he may be old but he knows what he's doin' as some o' these young fellers wouldn't know one end of a thermometer from a bottle of pills you can tell just by lookin' at them the way they . . . and keep an eye out for Nickie if I don't tan his hide first, I'm just gettin' the keys for the truck and you can . . ." She was halfway to the house.

I went over to Hud, who was standing shakily. "Want to lean on me?"

"I'm okay." Hud leaned a big hand on my shoulder, nevertheless. We took our time walking toward the truck. "Stay with Hud," I told Josh after Hud got up into the passenger seat. I headed for the house.

In the kitchen Ma was talking to herself about the whereabouts of the keys, her purse, and her glasses and whether or not she should take along the egg money just in case because you never know whether you're going to run out of gas. It provided a background that contrasted with my one, single thought: I had broken my own rule about not letting on I had a heart. Now I had a pain in it. I was involved. I felt not so much trapped, as tangled up in these other lives, a participant, not merely a captive audience.

"Just get going," I said to Ma.

She was still dithering about money. "I took most of it when I went into town that day. Monday was it no it must have been Tuesday and I took it in and deposited it in the bank in my egg account wouldn't you just know it no it must have been the Monday."

I said, "I have ten bucks up in my drawer; I'll get it. It'll be enough." I ran upstairs, pulled open the drawer where I had put the money under my maps and brochures, and saw at once that the money was there, but the black heart envelope containing The Woman's classified ad was not. I didn't have time to consider this. I grabbed the money, ran downstairs with it, and shoved it into Ma's handbag.

"I don't know what's to become of us," Ma kept saying over and over. "I don't know how we'd live without Hud. And that Nickie," she said. "I don't know what to do with him he's beyond me."

I could think of several things. Taking him out and stringing him from a rafter with twine sprang first to mind. "Hud will be all right," I said urging Ma through the door. "A strong, outdoor man like that!"

Outside Josh and I watched Ma climb up into the pick-up truck. She turned the key and after several attempts got the engine to roar. We watched the truck lurch past with

Ma at the wheel and Hud ready to grab it. Just before it pulled out of the drive, Ma got it to pause, rolled down her window, and called, "Get Josh to bed in good time if we're not back and make sure you get him to go to the bathr . . ." The car moved as if under its own volition along the driveway. At the same time, and perhaps subject to the same power as the truck, Ma's mouth, uncharacteristically, clamped shut. She adjusted her driving glasses and gripped the wheel like a kamikaze pilot. She grazed the mailbox on its post with the right rear fender but left it standing. Hud brought one hand up to his eyes.

I went in to turn on my computer.

Ma phoned to say Hud had to stay overnight in the hospital in Ambrose. They want to do tests on him. "His color's better," she said, "and he says he's fit as a fiddle now and intends to go home, but the nurses are going to tie him down if necessary, they say."

I can't imagine Hud all large and shaggy and sunburned lying in a hospital bed under snowy sheets surrounded by strangers with needles and scary machines. He'll be out of his element. He won't stay. He can't. He'll simply get better and never go back. Ma said she'd be home by-and-by.

She still wasn't home by Josh's bedtime, so I read him kerosene heaters, which he thought were right up there with snow blowers. I knew he would. He fell asleep halfway through radial arm saws.

Nick didn't put in an appearance until the truck pulled

into the driveway. I turned on the outside light and went to the kitchen window as soon as I heard it. I watched Ma get down, close the door, open it, get back in to turn off the lights, and finally head for the house. Nick emerged from the shadows and went to her with lowered head. Ma stopped. I stood at the open window.

"I didn't mean to," Nick wailed, his voice high and thin. "I didn't hurt the cat; I was only pretending."

Ma said, "I've tried so hard with you I've just tried and tried and you know I have but you've struck me a deep blow m'lad that pains to my very heart and soul when it comes to Hud as it did this day and if you were to be the death of him I'd wilt, I'd just wither and wilt for I'm only a bit of something growing on top of the earth but he's my root my very root and all I have in the world for I never was able to have any babies which I dearly would have loved and Hud too but he said it's all right m'darlin', it's all right don't worry there's lots of babies can't have parents so there now the very root of me so he is."

I'm turning off my machine for the night because my keyboard's getting all crusted up. Tears have a lot of salt in them.

CHAPTER

9

Ma phoned the hospital at nine o'clock this morning. All three of us foster children were in the kitchen, listening. I sat with an untouched bowl of cereal in front of me. Nick sat a little away from the table, fiddling with a box of toothpicks, his knee jigging up and down, never taking his eyes off Ma. I watched Josh slip silently off his chair onto the floor and sneak under the table. When I bent down to look, he put a finger to his lips and began casting spells.

"Aw-w-w," Ma said. She was talking to Hud in his room. "My soul, well. Is that a fact. Well, I'll be in to talk to them. Now you just do what they say Yes. Now you just . . . fine, they're fine . . ."

When she got off the phone, I asked, "Is he going to be all right?"

Nick stopped opening and closing the box of tooth-picks. Josh came out from under the table. Ma was silent.

"Ma?" I yelled.

"He didn't sleep a wink," she said quickly. "A special-ist from Ottawa comes once a week so they're keeping him in till the Tuesday and they're to have a look at him oh the doctor will have a good look don't you fear."

Ma looked at me then, woman to woman. A needful look. She didn't have to say anything. I just figured out what it meant. Something like, "We might need each other's support." I didn't feel like a foster child or a ward of the Children's Aid or even a hard-boiled Tess of the Tundra any longer.

Ma started taking everything out of the refrigerator. She opened lids, glanced into jars, sniffed at packages, and sorted everything, placing things on either the counter or the table. Nick never took his eyes off her as she moved back and forth from fridge to counter, fridge to table. She studied the food, not looking at anyone. Josh let two cats in, and she didn't say a word.

Watching Ma work, I felt this great weight in my heart. "Do you want me to help you?" I asked.

"No dear no it's all right it's just something I feel needs doing at this time and I'm the one that knows what's here and what should be kept and what should be pitched . . ." She looked into my face as if she could read minds. "Would you like something to do though for I think some-times it's good to be doing something as sometimes the job takes over the mind and I think I know what would suit you so I do." She took a bag of onions out from under the sink. "Peel these and slice them thin and I'll make cheese and onion pie for dinner and take some to Hud if he's allowed as it's his favorite so turn on the cold water tap and let it run for it helps."

I peeled and sliced and shed tears over the kitchen sink for the next half hour. I blinked at the ceiling and the four walls and went through half a box of tissues blowing my nose, and kept right on shedding tears. When the ordeal was over and the onions were placed in a bowl covered by a plate, I felt better. I looked terrible.

There was something I had to do. Ma's job was finished, and she'd gone out to the sheep and the hens. The boys were somewhere else. I looked up the number for the Ambrose hospital and dialed it. "Hud?" I said after I was put through to his room.

His voice sounded different over the phone. "Yep."

"Did I wake you up or anything?"

"Nope."

"It's Sara."

"Thought so."

"What did they find out was wrong with you?"

"Not much." He was about as communicative as usual.

"Hud?"

"Yep?"

"I was wondering if you'd be able to teach me to drive the truck after I turn sixteen?"

I had to wait for a reply. At last he said, "I think I'd be able to do that."

"Thanks, Hud."

"You're a grand lass, Sara," he said, and his voice cracked a little. "Salt of the earth."

It's very late. There was an eclipse of the moon tonight and I stayed up to watch it. At first the moon seemed to be disappearing, piece by piece. I was so sad I nearly cried (a habit I seem to be getting into). And then, the strangest thing! The moon became a sphere. A ball. Not just a flat disc hanging in the sky. It took on another reality, which cheered me up. It's very late now, and the moon is getting back to normal. I'd like to tell Ruth how I felt about the moon, but better not. Wouldn't want to throw her into a state of total confusion. She's at Bellcroft. She had a hot date with Grainger tonight. Dinner. Probably at the Ee-lite.

There is no significance to this whatsoever, but I'm going to give it to this insatiable machine to digest. When I was outside on the porch steps moon-watching, Edith-Ann ambled up to me, sat beside me, and put her chin on my knee. I held my breath and patted her. She looked up at me. I scratched her behind the ears and she just kept looking at me, her mouth open, her tongue halfway out. No growls. No bared teeth. But, good Lord, her breath!

This has been a day of darkness. If the sun shone, I didn't see it. This morning they took Hud by ambulance to Ottawa for an emergency operation on his heart. Ruth came right over. Ruby McKericher drove Ma to Ottawa; Ruth is staying here until tomorrow and Mrs. Oaksi has offered to come and stay after that if necessary. What else can I say?

Once I was stirring soup in a pot on the stove with a metal spoon. While I still had the spoon in the soup I touched a faulty control dial to turn down the heat. I got a shock. It was just a mild one, I guess, but it stunned me, jarred and frightened me and hurt in a way I can't describe. That's how I feel.

Ruth and Ma had a long talk while they were waiting for Ruby to get here. I can imagine what it was about. All Ruth said to me was that of course Hud will be all right. Modern medicine, blah, blah, teams of specialists, blah, nothing to worry about. Right. I feel so reassured.

One thing I know and Ruth knows too, there will be changes. Ma can't run this farm and a bunch of kids as well. Ma told Ruth she was applying to keep us foster kids no matter what.

I blew air out through my lips. Right. Here we go again. If Hud is not all right, the reality of the situation, as Ruth and I both know, is that Josh will likely go back to the Children's Aid, Nick, too, of course, and as for me? Well, I don't know. Inuvik has a nice sound to it. It's pretty far north. And west.

Something to think about. Or The Woman. Maybe it's because it's the middle of summer, but all I can see is green and brown and corn-yellow. White has been deleted. I don't seem able to set myself down on the windswept tundra as easily as I used to. I should be hardening myself against the worst. I should be sealing up my glass box before any more essence of Sara Moone escapes and mingles with this Huddleston atmosphere. I should not be sitting here thinking about Hud. And fear. What if he's afraid? If Hud crumbled, would the world end? I'd like to stop thinking about the way Ma grabbed me when Ruby drove in, and squashed me against her even though I was hard as a block. And she let me go. I want to stop remembering how I yelled, "Ma!" and ran after her and how when she waited for me, I bent and hugged her back. But I can't.

Hud has no descendants. No one to inherit his subtle strength. I'm afraid the world *would* end.

We go on, one day at a time. Hud came out of the operation pretty well. The doctors say we have to wait and see. Ma goes back and forth between here and Ottawa. Mrs. Oaksi stays sometimes. We don't really need her, although we want her. Her English is coming along. If she thinks we don't understand her, she says it louder. She sings all the time. We can't understand the words, but they sound comforting. They fill the empty spaces. Josh, the poor little sucker, thinks everything will be fine. No idea what's in store for him if everything isn't fine. Must be nice to be so inexperienced and so trusting. Matt comes over to help out on the farm. He says he doesn't want to be paid; he got his scholarship. He just wants to help out. Everybody helps. Fran sends food. Ruby and Pearl take turns driving Ma to the hospital in Ottawa. And Vern drops in once in a while to make sure we're doing everything right.

Edith-Ann has gone away. The strangest thing. Ma saw her ambling out toward the mailbox, which she often does, but this time she didn't come back. We've taken turns calling her. Ma went around half the township in the truck looking for her, but no luck. We miss her. Strange thing to say when you think about her. She didn't exactly typify man's best friend. Or woman's, either. But still, she had a presence. Old Vern said what we need is a good sheep dog and he could get one for us if we want. Ma said not yet.

Nick is leaving. He's the first. His social worker feels he's too much for Ma to handle on her own with Hud so sick. There have been phone conversations with the Children's Aid and the social worker has been to visit. Ma is upset and feels she's failed Nick in some way. The day she told Nick that he needed more than she and Hud could give him, tears ran down her cheeks. She told him that in the city there were people trained especially to help kids sort out their troubles, help them get turned around and heading in the right direction. She put her arms around him and held him tight. When she released him, he arched stiffly away from her, his eyes like green glass. "I guess I'll start packing," he said.

Josh was shamelessly enthusiastic about Nick's packing. He raced between the dresser and Nick's duffel bag with armloads of underwear and socks, comic books, tee shirts. Ma had to take him in hand, finally, and asked me to oversee the operation.

I took a patterned shirt off a hanger and began to fold

it. This was something I'd had practice doing. Nick sifted through some odds and ends of junk in a box from under his bed. He didn't glance at me, not even to leer. I looked in his direction once or twice, but it was as though I no longer existed as far as Nick was concerned.

"Hey, Nick," I said.

"What?" He still didn't look up.

"I'm sorry you have to go someplace else." What a lie! No, not entirely a lie. I was sorry to see a kid doing what I'd had to do so many times, put my meager life into a bag, layer by layer. I must admit I wasn't sorry he was leaving here.

"Don't matter to me," he said. He kept on rattling the stuff around in the box. "This place stinks anyway It's boring." He still didn't meet my eyes, but I could see his jaw muscles clenching and unclenching. I knew what he was straining to prevent happening. I had never cried when I left a place. Not once.

"Maybe you'll get assigned to Ruth."

"Who cares?"

"She does. She's the kind of person who cares about what's going on inside your head."

He stopped shoving the stuff around in the box and just stared at it. I tore a corner off a piece of paper on the desk and wrote on it. "Here's her phone number." I held it out to him, but he only eyed it quickly and looked away. I put it down on the bed beside him and went on folding shirts. Out of the corner of my eye I saw him pick it up, read it, fold it, and put it in his pocket.

By the time a man from the Children's Aid came to pick him up, it was pouring rain. Everybody had said good-bye to him. Ma had handed him a bag of apples and a dozen bran muffins to tide him over and the car was pulling out of the driveway when I remembered some unfinished business. I ran after the car yelling, "Nick! Wait! Nick!"

Ma, with tears in her eyes, had gone back inside, taking Josh with her. I splashed through puddles, yelling at the driver to stop. He noticed me as he paused before turning onto the road at the mailbox. He stopped the car and rolled down a window. I went to Nick's side of the car and motioned to him to roll down his. "Sorry," I said to the man, "I nearly forgot. He's got something of mine."

Nick looked surprised.

"That thing you took out of my drawer. I want it back."

"What thing?"

"That heart. That black heart with writing on it. It had something inside. A newspaper clipping. What did you do with it?"

"I didn't take nothin'." His face was pink, as if he knew I knew he was lying. "Let's go," he said to the driver.

"Don't go!" I commanded. Rain plastered my hair against my cheeks, and I scraped it back.

The driver looked from one of us to the other, unsure of what to do. "Do you want to get in out of the rain?" he asked me.

"No, I just want my clipping back. I know he took it. It was important. I have to have it."

Nick stared beyond the windshield wipers into the pelting rain.

"Okay," the man said. "I guess we'll have to get your stuff out and go through it just to make sure you haven't by accident got this clipping, Nick. Go get your bag out of the trunk. You can open it in the backseat." He turned off the car engine.

Quietly, Nick said, "I haven't got it."

"What's that?" the man asked.

Nick looked at me now. "I haven't got it."

In Nick's eyes I noticed something resembling regret, and instantly I felt an icy dread. I knew the answer to my question before I asked it.

"I gave it to that woman. She was in the Elite Cafe a while ago asking around about her daughter and going on about an ad she'd put in the paper. I finally gave it to her." His voice dwindled into a stammer as he turned to face me.

I backed away from the car. "Why?" I asked through the rain.

"To get rid of you." His voice was high with anger. "You come in here, you think you're so cool. You get Hud always letting you do things, giving in to you and everything. And Ma. You just spoiled everything for me. That's why. You just spoiled the whole thing."

The social worker interrupted, "If you haven't got that clipping, Nick, then I think we'd better go. We have a long drive." He turned the key in the ignition and the engine hummed.

I held up my hand. "Wait!" My eyes pierced Nick's and I saw him shrink back, away from me. I said quietly, evenly, "How did you know about the clipping?"

"You're not the only one in the world who knows how to run a computer. I know you inside out."

I turned and looked into the rain, seeing nothing. I felt as though I'd been stripped naked.

Nick was still talking. "I told her you had a copy of the ad and she got all excited, but it was taking her too long to come and take you away, so I gave her the heart thing for proof. I told her you asked me to because you were too shy."

I closed my eyes.

The social worker was drumming on the steering wheel. "You could settle all this over the telephone when we get there, you know. Here." He handed me a piece of paper. "Here's where you can reach him."

I put it in my pocket, turned, and walked slowly through the rain toward the little box on the hill. I didn't look up to admire the fanciful addition, the way it loomed out like the prow of a ship, as I sometimes did lately. I concentrated on putting one foot ahead of the other.

Rain is weeping down my windowpane. I've been sitting staring at my monitor screen. I didn't think I could even touch my machine again.

I see all the words are still here. I'm still here. Nick is the one who has gone.

Printed words are so present, so vulnerable. If I printed this stuff anybody could read my words, study them, give meaning to them. Concrete evidence that I exist. For somebody. I will never put this into print. I'd rather be something like a memory, locked safely into my computer. I'm pressing exit.

My machine is going again. I needed a change – to think out loud to someone, not something. I went downstairs, dug out the phone book, looked up the number, and scooped up the phone, trailing the cord after me into the coat closet. "Hello, Matt?" I said.

Three quarters of an hour later I was still shut in with the phone. Josh banged on the door once or twice, but I was able to ignore him. I heard Josh say to Ma in exactly Hud's tone, "Hasn't she been on that phone long enough?" And Ma replied, "She's a teenage girl you know and we're just going to have to get used to the fact as how well I remember the days of my girlhood oh the long talks Hud and me had to have and my father roaring 'Get off that blistering phone' but I never did for I liked to talk in those days . . ."

I felt a little better after talking to Matt. More or less. I got myself reassured that just because she has proof of a sort that I'm the one, it doesn't mean she can just drag me away by the hair, even though she now believes I want to go.

"I have rights. I'm almost sixteen," I said. I was going to add, "I can go up north and disappear if I want," but I wasn't sure that was what I wanted anymore. It seemed like a bit of a pipe dream now.

"Although the woman is your mother," Matt said.

"Maybe so, but . . ."

"Still, you don't owe her anything."

"Right."

"However, she is your own flesh and bl –"

"Quit it! She dumped me."

"I know. I was just thinking, that's all."

"Well, don't. It's not something you do well."

"Sara!"

"Sorry."

"I'm not. I think there's hope for me yet. I've noticed you only insult the people you like best."

For which I had no reply. Then he asked me to come over. He had to mind the shop because someone was arriving and his mother was out. I said I couldn't. My automatic response. I tried to soften it. "It's raining."

"It's stopped." I craned my neck around the closet door and saw that it was true.

"It's almost supper time."

"Come after. I'm free then."

"I promised I'd keep an eye on Josh."

"So bring him."

"Josh?"

After supper Ma said of course we could go and gave us our final instructions, which threatened to take up the entire allotted time we were allowed to be away. "And make sure Josh minds his manners for he knows how to say his please and thank yous as good as any of them but shouldn't he come back in and go to the bathroom for it'd be a shame if he . . ."

We were waving good-bye and disappearing into the barn where the bicycle was kept. Josh was all excited about being taken to Matt's house until he saw our method of transportation.

I wheeled the bike out. Josh, all scrubbed and slicked down, said he didn't know how to ride a bike, and I told him he didn't have to. I leaned it against the wall and wedged him into the crate strapped to the back. When I had straddled the bike I looked back at him. He had his mouth bunched up and was eyeballing the distance to the ground. "I'm walking," he said and tried to unfold himself.

"Relax," I said. "Enjoy it while you can because the next vehicle I drive will be Hud's truck, as soon as he gets home to teach me how." That gave him something to think about. And talk about. He spent the entire ride telling me that driving a truck is easy. All you have to do to drive a truck is change gears. And get your feet to reach the pedals. And watch where you're going. Another one – born to instruct.

At the Bellcroft sign we dismounted and walked down the tree-shrouded lane to the house. The recent rain still clung to the overhead branches, allowing tentative drops to surprise the tops of our heads. It was as dark as dusk winding through the woods. Small unseen creatures scuttled to safety under low-lying junipers. A partridge scared us half out of our wits as it flew up suddenly from the side of the road into the underbrush with a frantic beating of wings. I nearly dropped the bicycle; Josh reached out and hooked two fingers through my belt loop. "Pinch me not," he called out to the woods in general.

Changes had occurred at Bellcroft. The veranda and front of the house and half of one side had a fresh coat of paint. The front door had a screen in it. Matt, smelling of turpentine, greeted us. The house had given up some of its musty dampness to summer warmth and fresh paint.

"I wanna go out," Josh said as soon as we got inside. So we went out. I asked Matt about three of the trees standing guard over the house. They had orange X's painted on them.

"They have to come down," he said. "They're dying and could blow over in a strong wind."

"I wanna touch the lake," Josh said. So we set off for the boathouse. We saw Grainger sitting on the edge of the cliff overlooking the lake, scratching away at his yellow pad of paper.

"You'd save yourself a lot of time and money if you learned to use a computer, you know," I called to him.

He looked up. "I believe in basic elements," he said. "I believe that there is a definite link between the creative part of the brain and the hand that wields the pen. Besides," he said, "I can't decide which kind to get."

We made our way through the wispy grass behind the chipped and broken asphalt of the tennis court to the boathouse. Matt, with Josh bobbing importantly at his side, reached it first. I stood in the doorway, adjusting my eyes to its dimness. Resting on logs spanning one of the boatslips, we could see the hull of an enormous launch under its canvas shroud. Matt threw back a corner of the canvas, showing off its mahogany splendor. "*Lapwing*. That's her name. Isn't she a beauty?"

It was beautiful, all right. I had never seen anything like it, except in pictures. "What an engine it must have!"

"Someday, before dry rot takes over completely, I'm going to get her back in the water."

The past catching up to the future.

"I wanna go fishing," Josh said.

Matt untied the rowboat moored in the other slip. It leaked, but not badly. He took a faded life jacket down from a hook. He brushed off the cobwebs and old cicada shells and forced it onto a resisting Josh. He asked me if I could swim.

"Sort of," I said.

He reached into *Lapwing* and pulled out another life jacket. "Wear this," he said. "It will sort of save you from drowning."

"I don't need that."

"What would you do if you fell in?"

"Good Lord." I put the thing on.

Pulling hard on the oars, Matt rowed us along the shore. He rowed vigorously, as if reaching for a goal, a finish line. The only ripple on the still lake was the V formed by the boat's forward motion. Josh fished, sitting on the bow, straddling it. He had Matt's fishing rod, which he pronounced almost as good as the ones in the catalog.

He didn't catch much – a couple of weeds and a lily pad – but they seemed to satisfy him.

I sat facing Matt but decided to study the water's depths. Then I watched the sinking sun, between layers of cloud, gild the tops of distant pines. I could feel Matt looking at me. I turned from the sunset and he turned quickly to look over his shoulder, checking our course.

"I'll miss you when I go away to school," he said, still looking away. He stopped rowing and turned around to help Josh land a lily pad that was showing signs of putting up a fight. He looked at me then. "I won't see you until Thanksgiving." He kept looking at me as if he expected me to say I'd miss him, too. I've never said that to anyone before.

I cleared my throat.

He said, "Pardon?"

I said, "Maybe I'll write you a letter. I'm better at writing than talking." I think I am. In a letter I could tell him that when he smiles at me I feel as though the sun is shining only on me.

He was smiling at me.

I could feel myself melting and smiling back.

I didn't turn away and neither did he. I liked the way his hair slanted spikily to one side, and I liked the angular bones of his face. Along his jaw I could see little bristles of beard in the rays of the setting sun.

"I have to go pee," Josh said.

Reality Matt pushed hard on one oar, pulled with the other, and we turned back.

The sun was lower, casting a pink wash across a cloud-streaked sky. The vapor trail of a jet sliced a silver arc disappearing into the horizon. Below, on the lake's surface, minuscule water skaters slid tirelessly, randomly, heedless of our boat, bustling importantly back and forth on their flat little world.

Back in the boatslip Josh grabbed the rope tied to the bow and scrambled out. I gathered up his fishing pole and his lily pads and put them on the catwalk. Matt reached out his hand to me. I gave him my hard-boiled look, but he just kept looking at me with these soft, crinkling eyes. So, like some dorky fairy-tale princess, I took his hand.

Josh took a leak in the bushes and then caught up to us as we walked up to the house. Matt had my hand again. I didn't mind. I didn't even mind the way our shoulders kept bumping and the way our arms were touching as we strolled along. I guess you can get used to that sort of thing. And our fingers, interlaced.

We saw Grainger standing on the veranda and moved apart. "That woman was looking for you," he said to me. "You know, the one who's been staying here?"

"What did she want?" I asked abruptly.

"I don't know. She said she wanted to talk to Mrs. Huddleston and asked for directions to the farm." Grainger looked at me closely.

"We have to go," I said to Josh.

"Whater ya mean?"

"Is there anything I can do, Sara?" Grainger asked.

I looked at him. "Yes. Convince The Woman not to try to resurrect old ghosts."

"I don't understand," he said.

I grabbed Josh by the hand. "Phone Ruth. She'll tell you all about it. Come on," I said to Josh. "Ma wants us home before dark."

Matt said he'd come with us, and Grainger said he could borrow the car. I shook my head and set off, pulling Josh toward the bike.

"Sara!" Grainger called after me. "I don't know what's up, but if I can do anything to help you, I will. You can count on me."

I turned briefly and looked at him. If I was going to classify him as anything, I would call him a kindhearted man. I thanked him.

"What's the matter?" Josh asked. I pulled the bicycle away from the weeping willow without answering. "Wait up," he said. He stumbled along behind me in the dusk as I rolled the bike briskly up the lane into the wooded area. I had no plan, only the feeling that I couldn't put off a decision any longer. I had to choose: Either take a chance on the Huddlestons still being there tomorrow and tomorrow and tomorrow, or have the absolute certainty of this woman linked to me by flesh and blood, genes, ancestors. A mother who makes indestructible flowers.

Fireflies winked like some many-eyed beast. Josh wasn't with me. I stopped to look back. I could barely make out his stubby figure in the gloom. I heard his breath become louder and faster, until it burst from him in a long, loud bleat, like one of Hud's lambs. I put the bike down and went back for him.

I picked him up and managed to get him to fold himself into the wooden crate while I held the bike. I walked it out to the road while Josh sniffed and called out hopefully, pitifully, "Ma." I got on the bike at the paved road and began to pedal toward the farm.

We moved swiftly. My hair, made kinky by the drenching I'd had earlier, flew out from my head like a burning bush. Tears rolled slowly down my cheeks, and I brushed my eyes across the shoulder of my shirt. I talked to myself, sometimes out loud, in spite of Josh, sometimes only in my mind.

There was no escaping the fact that The Woman was my mother. I could hardly impose myself on the Huddlestons if I had a mother who wanted me. "Needed" would be the word. The Woman had hunted me until she'd tracked me down. She would be unlikely to give up the chase just because I had made the big mistake of getting attached to the Huddlestons.

I felt weighted down. Relatives, aunts, uncles, cousins, old Uncle Horace's bad temper, Great Aunt Hattie's nose. Nothing uniquely mine. I stopped at the intersection to let a camper go by and remembered hearing only of Aunt Bella. Nevertheless, there were probably others, strings of ancestors, clusters, all related flesh and blood, dead and buried. And then reason set in. In actual fact, the ancestor thing was true no matter what – whether I was a ward of the Children's Aid, adopted, or a bona fide member of a living family. Everybody comes from somebody. Lives and lives of people stretching back to the beginning of time, back to the cavemen. Adam and Eve were drowned and who was saved?

I hadn't asked for any of this. I had never cared who I was or where I had come from. I wished I'd dropped off the moon and had just happened to land here. I wished I could go back to the moon and stay.

It was barely light by the time we wheeled into the driveway. She was there, just as I knew she would be. I recognized the car out near the mailbox, small, immaculately clean.

"Someone's here," Josh said, his voice tinged with fear. "It better not be my mother."

"It's not your mother. Don't worry."

Under the outside light, he looked relieved.

"It's mine." I took a deep breath and held it as if I were in danger of going under.

We went quietly through the front door. I could hear voices coming from the living room. Josh looked up at me, expecting me to solve this mystery, to explain what was going on. I dashed up the stairs, leaving him open-mouthed and ready to wail at the bottom. In my room, with the door shut, I lay on the bed, my arm flung across my eyes. My heart pounded, deafening me.

I thought the door opened. I waited.

"Did she punch you?" Josh stood beside my bed.

I leaned up on my elbows. "Go 'way, Josh," I whispered. Poor little sucker, I thought. He had a mother who waited until he was four years old to decide whether or not to ditch him.

"Where's it hurt?" Josh asked.

"All over."

He left the room but returned a few moments later with a box of Band-Aids. One by one he took them out of the box and peeled off the backing. He climbed up onto the bed and started sticking them on my arms and legs. I almost smiled in spite of my misery. "You turkey!" I said. He put one on my forehead and one on my cheek and I laughed out loud. "You're crazy!" He didn't stop until he had used every last one. I got up and looked at myself in the mirror on my closet door.

"There now," Josh said. He was on the floor again and stood back to admire his handiwork. "All better."

"I don't think it's going to work." I was serious again. I sat on the edge of my bed and Josh sat beside me, his short legs straight out in front. I looked at him and then looked down at the repair work on my arms and legs. "If I have to be related to anybody, I wouldn't mind being related to you, you little blister."

"Me too."

"Brother and sister," I said. "Pinch-Me and Pinch-Me-Not."

"Yep." He wriggled closer to the edge of the bed so his knees would bend like mine. Pensively, he swung them, one and then the other.

"Sara!" Ma was calling me. "Sara, honey!"

"What?" I answered.

"Come on down."

I began to go down, peeling off Band-Aids as I went.

"Don't do that!" Josh said. "The hurt'll come back."

I shrugged and went downstairs looking like a patchwork quilt.

The Woman stood blank-eyed just inside the living room doorway. She started talking before I reached the bottom step. "I've just been explaining to Mrs. Huddleston about how I've been looking for my baby." She stared me in the face. "I nearly gave up because I thought you didn't want me. Then that boy came along, what was his name, Nick, Jake, something, and gave me this." She started to take the black, shredded heart out of her handbag but put it back in when she glanced up at me. I felt cold and pinched. She noticed the Band-Aids and asked, "Are you all right?"

"No," I said.

"When the boy said you told him to give me this clipping, I thought you might be interested, but probably shy, like me." The Woman stopped, waiting for me to say something, waiting for a word of encouragement. "I gave you a chance to mention it, but you didn't."

"I'm sorry," I whispered.

"I'm sorry, too. You know, I've made certain choices in my life; some I don't regret, one I do. It would be nice to be able to go back, to do it all differently, to undo the mistakes. I guess that's what I thought I was doing. I found out you were living near Ambrose, so I just started asking around. I was eating my dinner one night in that cafe place.

I guess I got talking to the waitress about my baby, and the next thing I knew this skinny kid comes up to me and starts telling me about you." She looked hopefully at me.

I was having trouble getting enough air and kept trying to take big gulps of it. I had a vision of Nick raiding my computer. Ma stood near the window, her hands on Josh's shoulders to keep him quiet. Her eyes were resting sadly on me.

"I hardly ever get excited, but I nearly jumped for joy. This was my chance to start all over, I thought. But then I thought, it takes two to tango. I talked to you a couple of times, but you didn't let on there was any connection at all. It wasn't until a few days ago, when the boy brought me this, that I knew you knew that I knew. I mean –" She poked at the top of her open handbag.

I looked from the bag to The Woman's face. For the second time it showed emotion. Sadness dragged at the corners of her mouth, loneliness filled her eyes.

" 'Too late' is what you wrote on it."

Ma clearing her throat provided the only sound in the small room.

"But," she went on, "people do change their minds, and maybe you have?" There was a note of hope in her voice.

I looked down at the adhesive strips on my arms and on the backs of my hands. I was hurting even more, in spite of them. The Woman had just become a person with feelings. Alive. Vulnerable.

"I need time to think," I stammered. I took my own raw wounds, turned, and hurried up the stairs to the security of my tiny bedroom. I closed the door. I heard the front door close and the crunch of someone walking along the drive. I heard a car start and drive away.

I sat cross-legged on my bed, peeling adhesive strips from my arms and relishing each tweak as it pulled my skin. Josh was downstairs. I could hear him asking for two butter tarts – one for him and one for his brother, Sara.

Oh, brother!

Food was the furthest thing from my mind. The thought of eating made me dizzy. I lay back on my bed and tried to make my mind a blank.

I heard all the night sounds of the Huddleston household, so familiar you'd think I'd known them all my life. Josh resisting bedtime. The toilet flushing. The tap running. Ma saying, "And don't forget to brush your teeth." I heard Ma come to my door and go away again. She came back a little later and put her head around the door, but I pretended to be asleep. I heard the rain start up again, rattling gently on the tin roof over the porch on and on into the night. The only thing I didn't hear was Hud snoring.

The safest thing to do would be to roll over with my face to the wall, pull the sheet up over my head, and pretend there are no other people in the world. I curled up like a capital Q. For Question. Because what if there are?

The sun is rising in a washed dawn. I am still in a fog, but I wanted to store yesterday in my computer before it disappeared.

I didn't think I would have the strength to turn my machine back on, but I guess I had to. The phone rang just after I turned it off a few minutes ago. Six-twenty A.M. I knew what it meant before Ma came into my room to tell me about Hud.

CHAPTER

10

Days have passed since I last used my machine. This will be a bit disjointed. I see that I keyed in a lot of stuff about Josh and me going to Bellcroft and The Woman coming here and then the sun came up and the world stopped.

Well, I guess it didn't stop. Old Hud. Still keeping it going from wherever he is. He was a powerful man. His strength was so well hidden you didn't know it was there till later.

I went back to bed after Ma told me. I wanted to close my curtains against the sun coming up but didn't have the energy. I felt empty but didn't want anything to eat. It was as though I'd turned to jelly. I couldn't get up.

I dozed all day, off and on, and was vaguely aware of Ma coming in with a bowl of something steamy or a glass of something chinking with ice cubes.

I think I remember Ruth coming into my room in the afternoon, and talking and leaving and coming back and talking some more, telling me things I had difficulty concentrating on. "Don't try to make any decisions right now," I think she said. Decisions!

The funeral. Half the county came. Everybody giving Ma comfort. Ma silent, wilted, needing. She perked up every once in a while when she looked at me or Josh. She was like a lifeline passing the comfort she got along to us. I don't know how much Josh understands.

Hud in the coffin looked carved from stone. Did he know how I felt about him? On his grave we left a huge basket of flowers cut from Ma's garden.

That night, after the funeral, after everyone had left, long after the house had settled down, Josh crept into my room. He pleaded with me to let him sleep in my bed.

"There's no room," I said.

"There's lotsa room. I'm invisible."

"Oh."

He wouldn't settle down. He kept crawling down to the end of the bed to look out the window. He was fascinated by the nearly full moon. Frogs sang beneath it. Leaves, made silhouettes by it, rustled on the maple tree near the window.

"Lie down, Josh," I said.

"Look at the moon."

"I've seen a moon before. Go to sleep." I thought I could hear Hud across the hall softly snoring.

"I want a moon for my name, too."

"Maybe you should go to the bathroom."

"No. Come 'ere an' see the man in the moon."

"I'm too tired."

He kept it up, so I dragged myself to the end of the bed. Huddled beside Josh, I looked through the window. As plain as the nose on my face was the nose on the moon's face. This was comforting. Something that was supposed to be in place, was, in fact, in place. Josh leaned his head against me, and I didn't move away.

I woke the next morning with a raging headache and a slight fever. Ma hustled a still-sleeping Josh back to his own room muttering about flu germs and cold in the kidneys and didn't she just know I was coming down with a dose of something pale as a plate I was. At least I gave Ma something else to think about. She plied me with more cold drinks and more hot soups and even tried to tempt me with a small piece of carrot cake. I think I ate only enough to keep body and soul on friendly terms. I lay on my pillow, drifting in and out of dreams. I floated free of gravity somewhere between the moon and the earth. In one dream I thought I was inside a small, shiny car speeding toward the prow of a glass ship. I tried to yell and bang my fists to give some warning, but no one could hear me because I was inside my mother, inside the car. The crash woke me. I had knocked a glass of ice water from the bedside table. It lay on the floor, the water spilt but the glass unbroken.

Ma took my temperature every few hours. Sometimes it was normal, sometimes slightly above. She phoned Dr. Cornish, who said a mild flu was making the rounds, nothing serious. Phone back, he told her, if my temperature goes up.

I continued to lie in bed for another day or two, not quite sick but not quite well. Josh babbled at me from the doorway. He wasn't allowed in for fear of catching my germs. Sometimes I talked to him; sometimes I fell asleep.

"I have a new favorite book," he said.

"What one?"

He held up a seed catalog. "From Matt. He said you could read it, too. It's got tomatoes in it like the ones we got, and corn."

"Sounds good."

He ran into the room, dropped it on my bed, and ran out. I looked at it cover to cover and then dozed off. I dreamed that I held a kernel of corn in the palm of my hand and it grew.

I had other visitors. Matt came with a bouquet of wildflowers, purple daisylike flowers with yellow centers mingled with white lacy-headed blooms.

Grainger came. "I think you have emotional flu," he said. He sat on my chair and pulled philosophically on his chin. "I get it sometimes when events in my life bear down too heavily on me."

I said, "Maybe, but I doubt it. I don't get emotional. I'm hard-boiled."

"Everybody has emotions. Some people spend half a lifetime trying to control them. I expect your own mother is a prime example." Grainger obviously knew the whole story now.

My own mother, I thought. I couldn't handle that. I closed my eyes.

"I had a long talk with your mother," he said. "I heard about the boy, Nick, and his involvement."

I think he wanted to talk more about it, but I pretended I was falling asleep. He didn't pursue the subject.

"Do you have any more typed pages for me?" he asked.

"Only what's in the computer."

"Do you mind if I print it?"

"Grainger, I'm too sick to get up. Can't you wait?"

"I can do it. I'm not totally computer illiterate, you know, just bone lazy." He started the thing going. "Well, I mustn't tire you. I'll go." He stood up.

"Wait," I said. There was something serious I had to ask him. I asked him if he would tell me truly if he actually believed in ghosts.

He said, "Why would I not believe in ghosts? It's like asking if I believe in air currents or energy. The problem with you is that your imagination is trapped inside some kind of a box."

I went to sleep to the *whirr-thunk* of the printer printing and wondered vaguely why he had turned it on and then hadn't waited to take his manuscript pages with him.

The next day Ma came into my room, sad-eyed and dithery, to tell me that The Woman was downstairs and wanted to know if I was well enough to talk to her. She picked up an empty glass. I started to say no but knew that this conversation was inevitable. Ma patted my arm and nodded her head. She left the room still nodding her head, knowing how it was.

I pushed my pillow farther up behind my head when

The Woman came into my room. Larger than life, she hovered over my bed. I hauled myself up into a sitting position and asked her to sit down.

She moved the chair closer to the bed. "I won't stay long," she said. "It's all my fault. I really feel responsible for . . . for this." She opened her hands toward me in a helpless gesture.

"For me getting sick?"

"Well, yes, that and everything. I mean the shock. It must have been upsetting to have some woman swoop down on you out of the blue and claim you as a daughter. I wouldn't like it myself."

"Actually, my foster father died. That was the shock."

"Oh, I forgot, yes, sorry I'm really sorry."

I didn't say anything.

"Still, it's pretty hard, I guess, to realize you have a mother alive and well and floating around the countryside. I'd feel as though I wanted to keep looking in the mirror."

I looked carefully at The Woman. I felt like closing my eyes on her. Not only do I acquire an unasked-for mother, I get one straight out of the Twilight Zone. A second thought crossed my mind. I must be feeling better. My sarcasm was coming back.

The Woman waved a hand back and forth. "That sounds crazy, I know. I mean, I would want to keep checking to make sure I was still the same me that I was before."

I nodded. This made sense, somehow. "I guess I know what you mean." I welcomed *myself* to the Twilight Zone.

Josh barreled into the room, hurling himself onto my bed. "Her and me are brothers," he said to The Woman, narrowing his eyes, daring her to contradict him.

Ma came in after him to haul him back out. "He's upset something fierce," she apologized to The Woman with a squirming Josh under her arm. I could hear her lecturing him all the way down the stairs. "Don't be such a little blister upsetting the applecart like that what with Sara sick half to death with the weight of everything on her . . ."

The Woman continued to sit, staring through the window. Following her gaze, I thought I could see Hud trudging away from the end of the garden with a wheel-barrow. I raised myself a little higher and frowned. Mistaken. I decided I'd better get rid of this flu so I could get out there and get the work done. I think I knew how Hud must have felt and wondered fleetingly if it were pos-sible to inherit feelings from someone unrelated.

The Woman began talking as if no one else were in the room. She said, "I made a mistake once." She paused, then continued. "I gave away my baby. I can't figure out how that happened, how I made that decision."

Facing her, I settled down onto my side and tucked the pillow into my cheek. I tried to imagine the volcano of emotion that had prompted the decision. I couldn't. I couldn't picture The Woman as a young mother. I couldn't imagine the baby. My imagination refused to muddle my present self with that helpless being, the former baby. What this woman was offering me was a ticket to the past.

"You can see right to the horizon out there," she said,

standing up, moving aside one filmy curtain. "Endlessly sunny fields," she said. Her face looked dead, as though the concept bored her out of her mind. She was looking at me now with her empty eyes. "I was hoping it wasn't too late." She got up to leave, still looking at me. She seemed to be viewing me from a distance, as if through binoculars. When she went out, she closed the door.

I lost control. My eyes filled with tears, were flooded, swamped. I was caught up and swept away from myself gasping, choking, drowning. I bent over, hugging my legs tight to my chest and heard my own sobs until I became aware of a hand smoothing my hair, rubbing my back. I looked up to see Ruth and felt saved from the depths.

Ruth. In her green dress. She always seems to wear green. A woman with hair like dried corn stalks blowing in a breeze and wearing a green dress. That was Ruth. She was there in my room, wisps of hair teasing her cheeks, tucked behind her ears. It was as though she knew I needed to depend on this image, as though she understood my need for at least one small piece of continuity in my life. Her eyes drooped at the edges when she smiled.

My head felt about to explode. I wished it would. I lay back and rubbed at my eyes with the backs of my hands. We talked for an hour. Longer. The point Ruth emphasized, over and over, was that we have to live in the present. You can't relive the past or change it. And as far as the future? The future's for dreaming about. She said, "You have to separate yourself from those around you and look objectively at the situation."

"Separate myself? But –" Good Lord. I finally get to be a free agent and I find I'm tied, tethered, and bound to every living creature in the entire county.

"What will happen to Josh?" I asked Ruth.

"It looks as though he's going to be able to stay here, for a while anyway. As long as Ma has lots of help and support he could stay indefinitely."

"What will happen to me?"

"You'll be sixteen the day after tomorrow. It's for you to decide."

"How can I decide to give away my mother?"

"Feeling sorry for her makes it that much harder for you, doesn't it?"

I nodded. I'd never felt sorry for anyone before this summer, not even for myself. Then I thought of Hud's sad eyes when I had said I could leave when I turned sixteen, of Ma when Hud was in the hospital, the way she had looked at me woman to woman as if to say, "The time might come when we'll have to cope with life together." I thought of Josh and quickly looked down before I turned completely into something soft and runny.

"Poor Sara," Ruth said. "I wish I could decide for you. I know you've had your feelings crushed over and over again, and now, whatever you decide, someone's feelings will be hurt."

"I feel like I'm being mangled," I said. "Torn apart. Chewed up."

Ruth shook her head sympathetically

"And puked out."

Ruth stared at me. Slowly she nodded.

After Ruth left I got out of bed and rummaged through the pockets of the clothes in my laundry bag. I went into Ma's room, closed the door, and picked up the telephone beside her bed. I was going to make a long-distance call and I was going to make it in private.

I spent the next day in a white mist, studying the pattern on the wallpaper, the creases in the palms of my hands, the way the sunlight dappled my ceiling.

Time was passing. Space was occurring. In the early evening I leaned back against the headboard of my bed. I had just been nourished by a chicken drumstick and a variety of vegetables from the garden, all arranged temptingly on my plate by Ma.

My illness had left me feeling lighter than air. Only the bed covers prevented me from floating up to the ceiling. The food had warmed me inside and out. I felt as if I belonged to the evening sky beyond my window.

Matt had written me a letter. There was something formal and old-fashioned about it. It was comforting and comfortable and reminded me of old books about other lands in other times. "If you decide to go with the woman, I will visit you and you will visit me at school. What difference can a few hundred kilometers make?" I put my tray on the desk and slid back under the sheet.

What is distance? Nothing matters. What is time or space? And who cares, anyway? What difference does anything make? It's all one. Life just goes on. Turn the page and there's more of the same. Press the down arrow and scroll up the next screen. Fast-forward to the next song. Flick the channels. I lay flat and weightless, listening to nothing.

And then I was listening to something. A car door slammed. I got out of bed to look through the window. I could see part of The Woman's car, and I heard Ma's voice greeting her politely. Josh ran across the yard. I couldn't see well enough to make out what was going on, but I knew this was it. Confrontation time. I went downstairs. Passing through the kitchen, I paused at the window.

Ma was outside in her apron with Hud, who was running a hand back through his hair. No, he wasn't. Good Lord.

Josh stood well away from The Woman, who was leaning on the fender of her car. I was about to go outside when I heard her say, "I don't know how I could have made such a stupid mistake."

"It happens, I guess," Hud said. His hair stood up on end from the way he'd been raking his hand through it. It gave him something of a startled look. He bent down and rubbed Edith-Ann behind the ears.

Hud was not there.

I felt weak. I pulled a chair over to the window and sat down.

Ma was wiping her hands on her apron, as if she wanted

to wipe it right off. She didn't like going outside the kitchen in her apron. It was a thing she had about aprons. I wanted to smile at the look of them. Josh and Ma. They looked so natural, so perfect. So human. Josh stood there scratching his behind until Ma noticed him and tugged at his sleeve to make him stop. He gave her a scowl, but he stopped. He mattered. Suddenly everything mattered.

Ma said, "Did you want to talk to her, to tell her yourself?"

The Woman was still leaning against her car, holding on to it as if she were part of it, as if it were part of her. Edith-Ann ambled over to her as if she were going to put her head under The Woman's hand.

Edith-Ann must have come back.

The Woman put her hands behind her back. "No, no I don't want to bother her again. She's not feeling well. I wouldn't want to get her upset. Just explain to her about the mistake. It would be better coming from you. Of course it's the fault of the paper for printing the error, but I should have noticed it myself. But there you are."

"There you are," Ma repeated.

Where? I wanted to ask. Where are we? What error has been made? I stood up now, filling the window, straining to hear every word.

The Woman looked toward the house as if she had noticed a movement at the kitchen window. She looked back at Ma. "Sixteen's so grown up in many ways, isn't it?" she said. I waited for Ma to give a dissertation on the number sixteen, sixteen-year-old girls in general, and her own experiences as a former sixteen-year-old, but it was not forthcoming. Ma stood, head bowed, not even looking at The Woman.

She went on. "Sara Moone's a young woman really, isn't she? It's funny how I could have got the year of my baby's birth wrong, although, I'm sure it wasn't my mistake. Newspapers make mistakes all the time. My baby wouldn't be nearly as grown up as that. Not nearly. But still, tomorrow is Sara's birthday. The day and month are right, which is quite a coincidence when you think about it."

"True enough," Ma said. She stood planted back on her heels, rocking a bit, nodding, the way Hud used to do. Josh ran after one of the cats and caught him.

"So," she kept on, "I have something for her."

Ma looked up now, curious.

The Woman took something out of her handbag. "It isn't anything much, really. It's hard to know what a grown-up girl like that would like. It's just a key ring." Again, she looked toward the house. Even if The Woman were gazing right at me, I could not have commanded myself to move. "It's got a sort of thing attached to it. A heart, I guess. Well, it has a key on it, too."

"A key?" Ma asked.

"Well . . . yes. Who knows? She might take it into her head to visit me sometime, if she's ever down near Hamilton. And if I was out somewhere, I'd hate to miss her. You know. She could let herself in, if she wanted."

Ma was standing there, rubbing at the corner of her eye with a knuckle, nodding a little.

"So, I'm away off home now . . ." The Woman began but couldn't finish because Ma had grabbed her and folded her into a warm hug. The Woman took it, boardlike, bent practically backward.

I went numbly back up to my bed and didn't watch the hand-shaking ritual. From my room I could hear the good-byes and good lucks and The Woman calling out, "I'm sorry about your husband. I'll send you some flowers. White. Last forever." I heard the car back out onto the road and drive away.

Ma came up to my room after The Woman had left, to explain the situation. "I don't know about the newspaper making a mistake but wasn't it a lucky thing she thought to say it for . . ."

"I know," I interrupted. "I listened. It gave us both a way out."

If Hud had been there, he'd have squeezed my shoulder with his big hand and left without a word, likely. Ma let words balloon into the room, rising to the ceiling, bobbing into corners until my small space was as full as a party. She tucked me in and kissed me on the forehead. It wasn't so bad being kissed on the forehead by Ma. I didn't even wince. Ma closed my door gently and left.

Then Josh came. "Lemme in," he said, giving the door a kick.

"Go 'way, Josh."

"How come?"

"'Cause I'm asleep."

"Oh." I heard his footsteps recede and then return. "Y'are not," he said to the outside of my door, but I didn't reply. I waited until he'd gone away, and then I turned on my machine.

Grainger and Ruth have just left. The rest of the story is that Nickie telephoned The Woman at Bellcroft Manor and admitted to her that he'd lied about me, that he'd read what I'd written in my computer, and that I had even phoned Hud when he was in the hospital and told him I wanted to stay here. Who would have thought that Nick would be of any use to anyone? You just never can tell. Of course, my phone call to him may have had something to do with his change of heart. I think I sounded fairly convincing when I threatened to do damage to certain portions of his anatomy.

Today is my birthday I woke up just before dawn feeling well and alive and, I have to admit, glad of it. I got up, threw a sweatshirt on over my pajamas, and stepped into my moccasins. Out in the hall I could hear Ma's deep, even breathing. I heard Josh making little smacking sounds. He sucks his thumb in his sleep. I crept down the uncarpeted stairs, stumbling through the dark house. I was almost sure I heard Hud snoring, but I think it was the hum of the refrigerator in the kitchen. The kitchen floor creaked as I made my way to the new room Hud had built. Out there I could see.

The lopsided moon setting in the southwest glowed as

bright, almost, as day. The sun rising pinkly in the east tinted the horizon without illuminating it. I unlocked and pushed aside the sliding door. Outside, the dewy grass bit like ice at my bare ankles. I stood rooted between moon and sun, joined to the universe, part of the earth, connected to my family.

The moon provided the only light and I walked toward it. The shapes of things were not immediately recognizable. Right now, I thought, something could be anything. Everything around me was full of potential. I stopped and looked back at the little square house with its shiplike projection, sitting like a promise on the brow of the hill. I stood there memorizing the world, thinking that maybe I should return to my room and write about it. It was cool at this hour at the end of August, bracing. I began to walk back the way I had come. Behind me I could hear Edith-Ann padding along in my footsteps.

The sun had inched up high enough to provide some slight illumination of its own. My perception of things began to change. Objects became distinct. I could make out the wheelbarrow at the end of the garden and beyond it rows of corn turning from no color to gray-green to green. The wheelbarrow waited to be filled with corn, which waited to be picked. A busy day was approaching, things would be accomplished, deeds done. It was my birthday.

Grainger!

I came back to my room to tap away on my keyboard, finally got around to taking a look at the printer, and discovered what he'd done. He'd printed *my* stuff, not his! I just discovered it. I can't believe this! I'm embarrassed to read it. How could he do it? And for that matter, why? All these words coming back to haunt me. Why would I want to read all this ancient nonsense? I have to admit that I went to the trouble of putting it in order, front to back, but I'm not going to even look at it. I'll tear it up. Burn it. Take it to the lake and drown it. Or bury it in the garden.

Just shut up. I'd like to tell my brain to just shut up.
Right.
I can blank out people.
Wrong.

Josh was up. I heard him on the stairs. He sits on the very edge of the top one, wiggles off, and then whumps down each stair on his rear end. And giggles at the bottom. "Where did he ever learn that?" Ma asked once. I taught him, but I didn't mention it at the time. It's something I used to do when I was a kid.

I could hear Ma stirring now.

I looked at my pile of pages. I could put them in a drawer, I guess. Save them for the future. Relics of the past. Words are so present. Once you've written something you feel you can't let on you don't exist.

"Ma!" I heard Josh yell from the stairs. "Ma, I went and got stuck! Ma!" Sometimes when he gets near the bottom he likes to sit with his legs poked between the uprights supporting the stair railing. The little blister. I remember doing that, too.